Mr. Tea and the Bobbin' Body

(A Madeline's Teahouse Mystery)

by

Leslie Matthews Stansfield

For information, email **Cozy Cat Press**, cozycatpress@aol.com or visit our website at: www.cozycatpress.com

COZY CAT
P R E S S

ISBN: 978-1-939816-41-2
Printed in the United States of America

Book cover design by Scarlett Rugers Design
www.scarlettrugers.com

1 2 3 4 5 6 7 8 9 10

This book is dedicated with love and appreciation to
Kathie Giorgio, friend, mentor, and coach.
Thanks for believing even when I doubted!
You are a precious gift from God in my life.

What Reviewers Say About *Mr. Tea and the Traveling Teacup*

"If you are looking for a can't put down read with mystery, humor, action and a little romance,) then this is the book for you." —*Melinathereader.com*

"The author has laid a nice foundation for future installments. Will romance bloom? What will come out of Mr. Tea's mouth next? Who will be the next victim? Are there still ghosts lurking about? I am not so patiently waiting for Stansfield's next story." —*Escapewithdollycas.com*

"Amidst all the turmoil going on around them, Leslie Matthews Stansfield's characters are definitively fleshed out right from the start, very easy to fall in love with."— *nightreader-bookblog.blogspot.com*

"Darlings, be sure to steep yourself a nice pot of tea, scoff a biscuit or two for dipping, snuggle down by the fire with a blanket and read this wonderful first story in the Madeline's Teahouse Mystery series. The second book is on it's way and Yours Truly, can't wait!" —Barbara Jean Coast, author of *Strangled by Silk* and *Death of a Beauty Queen.*

CHAPTER 1

Putting on her robe, Terry glanced in the mirror, then stepped into her bedroom. A vision flashed through her mind. She stopped, turned around, and went back into the bathroom. Squinting, she stared at the mirror. A cold shiver went through her. She got closer to the mirror and looked very carefully. OMG! IS THAT A GRAY HAIR? It certainly looked like a gray hair. It wasn't there yesterday. At least she didn't think so. No, no, no! Her boyfriend Greg's high school reunion weekend started tonight. It simply couldn't be. *Breathe,* she told herself. She'd have to ask Karen, her sister.

Terry contemplated the gray hair. It wouldn't surprise her if it was the result of the recent mystery. Terry and her sister Karen had turned their childhood home into a teahouse. No sooner was it ready to open when things had started to go bump in the night. When the sisters came home one night to what appeared to be blood running down the attic stairs, the police had been called in. That was how Terry met her new beau, Greg Mullins. Uncle Henry and Aunt Rose, who lived next door, lent a hand as well. Aunt Rose loved a good crisis, and the "haunted" teahouse had her in her glory. Terry decided that she wouldn't be surprised if the gray hair was a direct result of the haunting and the harrowing events that went with it.

Forcing herself to be casual, she walked into Karen's bedroom. No Karen. A humming sound came from the attached bathroom. Terry went to the bathroom doorway and watched Karen putting on her make-up.

Karen stopped humming and cut her eyes to Terry's reflection in the mirror. "Good morning," she said. "Are you okay? You look a little pale. I hope you're not getting sick. I'm counting on you to help with things this weekend." Karen scowled into the mirror.

"I think I'm fine. I overate yesterday. I feel a little...whalish."

"Whalish. Nice word for the day after Thanksgiving. I like it. Whalish."

Be calm and breezy, Terry told herself. *Don't give it away.* "Hey, Kar, have you ever had a gray hair? I...um...think I saw one on Shannon yesterday." *Oh, nice; throw Shannon under the bus*, she thought, looking at her own reflection in the mirror. Shannon Dindle was their next door neighbor and lifelong friend who also helped Terry and Karen run their teahouse.

Karen frowned and studied Terry in the mirror. Then Karen turned and looked at her directly. "Do *you* think you have a gray hair?"

Terry was afraid to speak, to even blink. *If Karen knew, would she tell Greg? Would she make fun of her in order to seem cool this weekend?* Terry felt the tears spill over.

"Oh, honey, don't panic. I'm sure it's nothing," Karen cooed at her.

"I'm afraid Greg will be ashamed of me this weekend. I'll look old."

"Oh, please! He's older than you. He's my age, remember. Don't be silly."

"But he's so hunky, still. I don't want people to feel sorry for him."

Karen rolled her eyes. "Okay, you've been told forever how beautiful you are. The fact that you don't realize it is part of your charm. Trust me, really. Now, where is the little devil?" Karen said, stepping forward and studying Terry's head.

"Right here," Terry answered, looking in the mirror and pointing to the monstrosity.

"This one? This little thing? I think it's just blonde," Karen said, separating it from the others.

"Ow!" Terry yipped as Karen yanked the strand of hair out of her head.

"Problem solved!" Karen said, as she let the hair drift to the ground like a fall leaf. "All gone. No worries. We have to get going. We have to set things up for later. I can't believe Shannon convinced me to donate so much time, energy, and food to this shindig."

"I'll get dressed. I think it'll be fun. It'll give us a chance to show off our skills and Mr. Tea," Terry said, rubbing her head. Mr. Tea graced the parlor of the sister's business—Madeline's Teahouse—and charmed their customers with his wit and amazing vocabulary. In his previous home, it was rumored the bird was psychic. Mr. Tea had shown up just in time to help the teahouse crew solve their most recent ghostly mystery.

"Crud, I forgot we have to get him there, too. Ugh, one more thing to do."

"Just call Shannon and go over with her. I'll call Greg, and he and I can bring over what food you can't––and Mr. Tea."

"Fine, fine," Karen said, waving her arms in the air. "I never wanted to go to this thing. I hate these things. I detest them even more now that I'm divorced and childless. Hate, hate, hate. I didn't like half those people in high school, and now I have to pretend to be their long lost buddy."

"What are you talking about? You were popular in high school. You were in the theater group and the cheer squad. All I did was design scenery for the plays," Terry said, heading to her room with Karen on her heels. Terry started to get dressed as Karen said, "That was just it. You had talent. Everyone 'ooohed' and 'ahhhed' at what you did. I just sang in the back of the chorus."

Terry put on her shirt and stared thoughtfully at Karen. "You should count your blessings. Ya know, some people won't be there this weekend because they're dead. Mary Elizabeth died of breast cancer. Adam Weaver was killed by a drunk driver. Donna Wiggins' car went over that cliff. Speaking of the Wiggins, is Rachelle Wiggins coming this weekend?"

"Yeah, I think so. I'm pretty sure she was one of the names Shannon said. I remember Shannon talking about how hard it would be for Rachelle to come without her twin sister. Did you know Adam Weaver's parents donated over five-hundred dollars toward the reunion costs? I don't think they ever got over that loss."

"Greg told me the kid that hit him died a year later when his car flipped over in a snowstorm. He was drunk again. Okay, I'm ready. Are we going together or separate?" Terry asked as they headed downstairs.

"Call Greg and see what he wants to do."

The front door opened and Greg Mullins walked in. "Hello," he said, looking up.

"Right on cue. I think you and I will bring Mr. Tea and whatever Karen and Shannon can't fit in Shannon's van," Terry said.

"Nope, Tom and Shannon have already made two trips this morning. I was sent to collect you and Mr. Tea." Tom O'Hara, a police detective who worked with Greg, was Shannon's boyfriend.

"Secrets," Mr. Tea said, hopping around in his cage and fluffing his wings.

"Yeah, okay. Let's get a move on," Greg said, as he headed into the parlor to get the bird.

***

Terry, Greg, and Mr. Tea were manning the nametag table. People mulled about, drinks in hand. Terry glanced at her watch and was stunned to see it was almost seven. It amused Terry to realize that many of the men who were the hairiest teenagers were now bald or balding. She kept looking over at Karen as one woman after another pulled out pictures of children. Karen was always gracious. Terry liked being able to sit back and watch people. She was lost in thought about who was thinner, who was heavier, who was now more well-endowed than in high school, and who, much to Terry's amusement, brought a trophy wife or a boy-toy.

"Did I tell you how proud I am of you and the amazing job you did with the decorations?" Greg whispered in her ear, giving her neck a little nuzzle.

"Thank you," Terry said, feeling a hot rush run through her. "I don't think it's much, though, compared to all the cooking Karen and Shannon did. All those hors d'oeuvres! The waitresses keep running back to fill their trays."

"Well, the first hour is open bar," Greg said. "It's a really smart idea to have food. The doors should open for dinner in about fifteen minutes."

"I liked the idea of cocktails by the pool," Terry said. "I had fun doing the ocean cruise theme. Shannon really wanted the reunion to take place on a cruise ship. I did my best." She loved listening to the comments passers-by made.

"That ocean looks so real, I keep waiting for my feet to get wet."

"The way that mermaid's hair glows, you'd swear it was the sunlight shining on it."

"I had to look at the picture of the captain at the wheel for a few seconds to realize it was a painting. Look at the way his cap seems to catch the light! I heard Terry Sutter did the art work. No surprises there. She was always amazing."

"Well, look who it is!" a woman said, walking up to the table. "The famous set designer. Do you recognize your old friend, the costume designer?"

Terry gasped. Until the woman said, 'costume designer,' Terry didn't have a clue. Now it was obvious. "Wow, have you lost weight! You look great," Terry exclaimed, getting up and running around the table to hug her old friend.

"Gastric bypass and lots, and I do mean lots, of exercise," Sandra Hochberg said.

Terry turned to Greg and did the introductions.

Greg stood and shook Sandra's extended hand. "Honestly, I would never have recognized you, Sandra. Terry is right, you look great."

"Thanks, Greg. That's kind of you," Sandra said. Terry noticed her squeeze Greg's hand. Turning to Terry, she said, "Terry, I don't remember you being in my grade. Were you?"

"No, I was two years behind. I'm helping out. Karen, my sister, enlisted me," Terry said, realizing Sandra held onto Greg's hand a little too long. *Old friend indeed,* Terry thought. Perhaps at a high school reunion, all bets are off.

"Nice legs, toots," Mr. Tea said.

"Well, isn't he the charmer," Sandra said, winking at Greg.

"Yes, he's our macaw. We call him Mr. Tea, *t-e-a.* Karen and I own a teahouse now."

"I heard that. And I heard it's marvelous. My mother went with some of her friends. I hope to visit it this weekend."

"We'll be open tomorrow from eleven to three," Terry said. "We're keeping shorter hours this weekend so Karen can enjoy the reunion activities. Speaking of which, it's almost time to open the doors for dinner."

"Will you be stuck at the teahouse, holding down the fort?" Sandra asked, her voice sounding a bit hopeful.

"No, we close before the activities start," Terry said.

"Oh, goody. Anyway, Greg, I hope you and I can catch up over dinner and a drink or two," Sandra said.

"I'm sure there'll be room at our table," Greg said. "That would be great. Aren't the decorations Terry did fantastic, Sandra? She outdid herself." Greg smiled broadly. "I'm so proud of her. Have you noticed the details on the murals? Don't the waves look like they're about to break? Did you notice the mermaids on that island scene other there?" Greg asked, pointing. "What about the waiters and waitresses being dressed as sailors? That was her idea and the caterers loved it. The dining room is decorated like the deck of a ship, with railings and everything."

"Warning! Warning!, Warning!" squawked Mr. Tea. "Anchor's away!"

"That's interesting," Sandra giggled. "He's so precious." Then, with a rather cold look in her eye, she said, "So, are you two…together?"

"Sure are," Greg said. "Oh, I think I see them unlocking the doors to the dining room." He walked around the table and put out both of his arms. "May I escort you ladies to dinner? he asked.

"How lovely," Sandra said, her voice a little flat.

"We'll be back, buddy," Terry said to Mr. Tea.

"Here we go again," he said, hopping from foot to foot.

***

"That buffet was amazing," Tom O'Hara said. "I didn't think I'd ever want to eat after yesterday, but…"

"You always say you never want to eat again," Shannon huffed. "You're always eating and never gaining. It's downright annoying." She threw her napkin on the table in mock disgust.

"I think it's a man thing," Rachelle Wiggins-Taylor said. "My husband is the same way."

Terry really liked Rachelle. Karen had invited Rachelle and her husband, Russ, to join their table for dinner. Greg, Russ, and Tom really hit it off. Sandra seemed to be enjoying talking to Karen and Shannon about recipes.

"Terry, I really can't tell you enough how perfect these decorations are," Rachelle said. "I'd forgotten how talented you were. You and Sandra were so artistic. You made the plays that much better by your work."

"Let's not forget Donna's make-up skills," Sandra said. "She added a lot. I was so sorry to hear about her death."

"Me, too," said Karen.

"I still can't believe she's gone," Rachelle said. "Holidays are the hardest. My mom likes to pretend everything is fine, but there's always an emptiness at the table."

"I feel that way too since Karen and I lost our mom," Terry said.

"I think of how magic the holidays seemed as a child." Rachelle sighed. "My children love them. I never thought about how adults feel. It's like we try and put away our memories to let the children have their magic."

"I never thought about it that way, but you're probably right," Karen said. "That's quite insightful..." Karen's voice trailed off as they all turned their heads toward the sound of a commotion. It seemed to be coming from the doors by the pool area. That was when the screaming started.

CHAPTER 2

"What in the world?" Rachelle said, craning her head to see what was happening.

"Sounds serious," Russ added.

"Could be a prank," Sandra added with a shrug.

Terry saw Greg and Tom exchange looks. They excused themselves, and began to carefully pick their way forward through the growing crowd.

"Someone probably got drunk and fell in the pool," Shannon said. "We debated locking the doors to the pool once dinner was served. We decided to just keep the doors closed and then reopen them when dessert was served. I was nervous about just this sort of thing happening. Hopefully, whoever it is, is okay. I'd hate to have an accident ruin the festivities this weekend."

"At my high school reunion last year, someone got drunk and landed on the dessert table," Russ said. "I was so disgusted. It's not like we're in our twenties anymore. There comes a time to grow up a little."

"Well," Karen added, "some grow up very, very little. It's like high school was their glory days and they can't move past it. I find it a little sad."

"Did you hear that Bobby Cooper was just found dead in the pool with blood all over?" a skinny redhead said as she made the rounds, spreading the rumor.

"Mary Crowley was always one to get the scoop," Karen said.

"Mary Crowley!" Terry exclaimed, throwing her arms in the air. "I knew I recognized her. I just couldn't place her. She really hasn't changed much."

"Forget her," Karen snapped. "I wonder if Bobby really is dead."

Greg's voice came over the loudspeaker. "Ladies and gentlemen. There has been an accident in the pool area. The police have been called. We ask that you all stay calm and remain in the dining area. The hotel is making arrangements for another room for us to move to. Again, stay calm and wait for further instructions."

Tom appeared a few yards away from their table and motioned to Shannon who went over to him. He whispered to her for a few minutes. She came back to the table and excused herself. "Tom needs some information. I'll be back in a few," she said.

They sat in silence. Many around them were speculating, but Terry felt too shocked to move. She guessed the others at the table felt the same way. Terry watched as some people in the room seemed to revel in the incident, like vultures eyeing a corpse.

Suddenly, she felt her cell phone vibrate. She pulled it from her pants' pocket and looked at the text. *Ter, Kar not answering phone. Come to room 137 NOW.*

Slightly confused, Terry wondered if Shannon wanted just her or her and Karen. Turning to Karen, she asked, "Is your cell phone off?"

"Yeah. Why?"

"Excuse us for a second," she said to the others at the table. "Karen, Shannon needs us to help her out. We need to leave for a bit."

As they reached room 137, the door was slightly ajar and Shannon was standing outside. She waved them over. Terry could see a woman sitting on the bed, arms wrapped around herself, crying.

"That's Bobby's wife, Shantel. She's hysterical, and I'm not sure how to help."

"So…is Bobby really…" Terry said.

"Dead? Yeah. I'm not sure of the details. Something around the pool. Tom asked me to sit with her while they try and reach Bobby's parents. All I can get from her is something about blood. I don't want to ask her anything. I just sit there. The poor thing. I do know they have triplets. I feel helpless. Any ideas?"

Karen peeked inside, and then looked nervously at Shannon and Terry. Terry felt her heart break. *That poor woman could not be more distraught or lost*, she thought. Pushing open the door, she went in and sat down next to Shantel. "Shantel, Bobby was my friend in high school. I'm so sorry." She wasn't sure what else to say because she didn't know what actually happened.

Shantel turned and stared at her for a long moment. "He said he was going to meet an old friend for a minute. He was so looking forward to this weekend. Aren't you the girl who did the decorations? He said he knew you."

Terry felt a lump in her throat. "Yes, he was the only football player who would show up to help decorate the gym for pep rallies. He was very kind and had a good sense of humor. He wasn't cocky like some of the others."

Shantel smiled. "That was why I loved him. He made me laugh. He was always willing to help someone. I don't know why someone would want to kill him. I have triplets at home. How am I going to take care of them? They adore Bobby. He is…was so good with them."

"Kill him?" yelped Terry. "I thought he had an accident. What makes you think he was killed?"

The woman looked at her in shock. "I found him. He was gone quite a while. I went looking for him. I wandered into the pool room and there he was, floating in the pool, face down, with his head bashed in. I was going to jump in the pool, but someone heard me scream and grabbed me. That's the last I remember until I realized I was here."

At that moment, Greg walked in. He just nodded at Terry. She couldn't be sure, but he seemed…annoyed. Why would he be annoyed to find her here? She got up and left the room, closing the door behind her. She thought, *Good God, murder? Why?*

Shannon, Terry, and Karen walked slowly to the lobby. There, a hotel employee directed them to the ballroom. Everyone else was there, milling around. They looked as baffled as Terry felt. Rachelle wandered up to them. "They said Bobby is dead and no one can leave just yet. There are more police here. Bruce Wilson said he saw Bobby's body in the pool. There was blood around the pool and in the water. He thinks someone killed Bobby."

"What was Bruce Wilson doing by the pool?" Karen asked.

"He said that Bobby told him something creepy was going on and that he had to go find someone, or meet someone. Bruce wasn't sure. He saw Bobby's wife start to look for him and Bruce went to help. He was entering the pool area when she screamed."

Terry watched Shannon put away her cell phone. She seemed to be stifling a laugh. She scuttled over, grabbed Terry's arm and pulled her aside. "Okay, try not to laugh out loud," she said, smirking. "Tom called and said that Mr. Tea keeps squawking, 'Greg's a hottie.' Greg is fit to be tied. The other officers are now referring to him as 'Detective Hottie.'"

Terry put her hand in front of her mouth and closed her eyes. *Don't laugh, don't laugh…* She took a deep breath. "No wonder he seemed perturbed a few minutes ago. I thought he was annoyed with me. Wow, I've never heard Tea do that before. He's said the word 'hottie' when Greg's around, but…"

"Tom swears Tea's doing it to bug Greg. The bird says it and then gives his tail feathers a little swish."

"I love Tea, and he is smart, but I highly doubt he's that smart," Terry said.

"Hey, what's up?" Karen said, coming up behind Terry.

"Tom says he and Greg will be busy for a while. We're on our own," Shannon said, giving Terry a 'keep your mouth shut' look. Karen would definitely use the hottie remark to torment Greg. There was a commotion to their left. Terry turned and saw an older man arguing with an officer.

"That's Coach Walker," Karen said. "What's he doing here?"

The three women inched closer. It was hard to hear over the crowd. The coach's face was red. He was obviously furious. Bruce Wilson emerged from the crowd and walked over. A few police officers trailed behind him.

Terry was suddenly aware that she was extremely hot and crowded. Everyone was trying to get a better view. She turned to Karen. "I gotta get some space. This is too stifling for me. I need air."

"You go ahead," Karen said. "I want to find out what's going on."

Terry felt annoyed. "Really? Can't it wait? We'll hear it later anyway."

"Hey, don't snap at me! You're just as nosy as the rest of us." Karen straightened her body in a show of indignation.

Terry realized how ridiculous she must sound. She'd worked her way up with the rest of them. "Yeah, I'm sorry. I just can't stand feeling crowded and hot." She wiggled her way back to someplace less jam-packed. She closed her eyes and took a few wonderful deep breaths of spacious air. Just as she opened them, someone grabbed her arm. Turning in alarm, she saw Shannon.

"Let's go walk around the hotel," Shannon said. "It will be less crammed in the halls."

"Can we do that?" Terry asked. "I thought we all had to stay here.

"We probably should, but I think we can slip out for a bit. It's too hot in here for me."

Karen emerged from the throng and headed in their direction. "Coach Walker is screaming that someone called his house and whispered that Bobby was dead."

"That's weird," Shannon said. "Anyway, we need to get a break from the mob," she added. "Do you want to go for a walk with us, or stay?"

"I'll go," Karen said. "It's getting too hot in here."

"My thoughts exactly," Shannon said. "Let's find an exit."

They found an exit door in the back of the ballroom. It led to a small meeting room. They cut straight through to a hall of rooms.

"Why would someone call Coach Walker?" Terry asked. "How would they have his number?"

"I have no answer for either question," Karen said.

"That's creepy," Shannon added. "It was probably an old team member who didn't want to get involved."

"I feel so bad for Shantel," Terry said. "I can't imagine going through that. How awful to find your husband dead like that."

"Did I hear her say Bobby told her he was going to meet someone?" Karen asked.

"Um, maybe. Yeah, I guess that's what she said. I don't remember, but that sounds right. Now that I think about it, I think that was why she got up to go look for him."

As the three walked in silence, Terry thought about her own fears. Seeing so many people her age with families made her wonder where all the time went. She wondered if she had wasted time in past relationships. What if the relationship with Greg didn't work out? It seemed great, but one never knew.

At an intersection between halls, they almost collided with Bruce Wilson. "Whoa! Geeze, sorry. We're going to my room for some drinks. What are you ladies doing wandering about?"

"Getting air," Karen said.

Bruce was not alone. Coach Walker and Chris Miller were with him. "The police said it would be okay if we hung in Bruce's room, so here we are," Chris said.

"I need a drink," Coach Walker said.

Terry thought it looked like he and Chris already had quite a few drinks. Bruce's hands were shaking so badly that he could barely hold the key card.

"Hey! Come hang with us, you beautiful ladies," Chris said.

Terry didn't think this was such a good idea, but if anyone knew what was going on, it was these three. She looked at Shannon and Karen. They seemed to be wavering as well.

"I could use a chance to see if I need to get Mr. Tea," Terry said.

"Mr. Tea?" Chris asked.

"My Macaw," Terry said.

"Oh! That really funny bird that was there when we checked in?" Bruce asked.

"That would be him," Karen said.

Terry took a moment to look around. They were in some type of suite. The beds were in an adjoining room, and they were standing in a living room. It was done in a mauve tone with blue and gray shades and patterns. The rug was mauve. The walls were off white. The tables had mauve tiles. *Hotel chic,* she thought.

"Nice room," Shannon said.

"Yeah, I decided to get a suite," Bruce said.

"We were gonna enjoy the weekend," Chris said. "We were gonna be the three amigos again, the great football threesome." His voice caught. He stared into space.

Terry took out her cell phone and texted Greg. "*I'm in room 156. With Kar, Shan and Bruce and Tea.*

"C'mon in and have a seat," Bruce said, waving them in from the doorway.

It seemed very odd to be in a hotel room with three men.

Karen regained her composure first. She walked over to Coach. "Coach Walker, you probably do not remember me. I'm Karen Sutter, that's my sister Terry on the right, and Shannon Dindle on the left. Sorry to see you again under these circumstances."

"Yeah, it's so friggin awful," Coach said. "I just can't believe this."

"I don't think any of us can," Bruce said.

The door swung open and Tom came in with Mr. Tea.

"Party's here," said the bird.

"What in God's name…" Coach started.

"It's our bird," Terry said, taking the cage. "That was fast," she said to Tom.

"I was right next to his cage when Greg called me."

"Is it okay for us to be out of the ballroom?" Shannon asked, clearly worried.

"It's fine, for now," he said. "We just need to know where people are. A few other people have even gone to their rooms. I'll call ya later," he said as he left.

Terry put Tea on a nearby gray glass table. "Meet Mr. Tea," she said to Coach.

Coach didn't seem to hear her. He now looked like a main character in a horror show. He was pale, shaking, and clearly bewildered. "I…I answered my phone. The caller ID said, 'unavailable'. A voice whispered, 'Bobby Cooper got what he deserved. Pay attention. You're all guilty.' Then she just hung up. I tried Bobby's cell phone. We were supposed to get together this weekend, all the guys from the team that year. I couldn't wait to see them. After the call, I kept trying Bobby's cell and he never picked up. I had to know. Oh, God." Coach Walker began to wobble. Bruce grabbed his arm and helped the man sink into a nearby couch.

"Danger," squawked Mr. Tea.

"No kidding," said Coach, rolling his eyes.

"Grumpy Gus," said Tea.

"Damn bird," retorted Coach.

Mr. Tea simply raised his tail and pooped.

Terry looked out the sliding glass doors. It seemed so peaceful out there. "Let's get some air in here," she said, sliding the glass doors open. She stepped onto the balcony. The stars were beautiful. There was a low rumble of noise from all the people in the hotel. The parking lot was full with cars. Somewhere within the hotel, a band was playing. She could hear the thump, thump, thump of the drums. Of course, there were other functions going on, untouched by this ugliness. The hotel was full, not only with people for the reunion, but other groups. The reunion group was due back tomorrow for a fall fling. That was what the dances were always called in school—flings. Suddenly, she felt exhausted. She was supposed to be back here in just a few hours to help decorate, again. Maybe they'd cancel the dance. Her phone vibrated and Karen stepped out on the balcony. Terry pulled her phone out and looked at the caller ID.

"Rose," she said to Karen. "We must have made the eleven o'clock news. Hello?"

"Terry, dear, are you all alright? The news says there was some type of accident where a man was killed. The newsman said it happened at the reunion."

"Yes, Rose, we're fine. Bobby Cooper was killed. I really don't know anything. Greg and Tom are here, working. We'll be fine."

"Okay, Dottie is here with me, and we wanted to make sure. Take care of yourselves and call in the morning," Rose said.

"Will do. Thanks for checking on us, Aunt Rose." Clicking her phone shut, Terry said, "Oh, yeah, we made the news." The sisters angled to try and see the front of the hotel. They couldn't. They wandered back in and sat at a table with mauve and gray fabric-covered chairs.

"There's a coffee pot over there. Would anyone like some coffee or tea?" Shannon asked.

"I'd love a cup," Coach Walker said. "Do they have any booze to put in it?"

Everyone looked around. Bruce got up and looked next to his side of the couch where he sat. "Voila, mini bar!"

"Do you think we should use that?" Terry asked. She sure wasn't going to pay for it, and she wasn't sure Bruce was thinking about the cost.

"I'll cover any cost. Just throw something in the coffee, will ya, Wilson? I'd be much obliged," Coach said.

Shannon went to the coffee station with Bruce at her heels. There was a knock at the door. Terry opened it to see a young woman dressed in black slacks and wearing a shirt with the hotel name and logo on it.

"Some sandwiches, compliments of the hotel," the woman said. "Can I get you anything else?"

To Terry's surprise, Karen piped in, "Yes, some hot cocoa, Kahlua, and whipped cream. It could be a very long night."

"Kar!" Terry said, feeling like they were taking advantage.

"Oh, for the love of pizza," Karen said. "Relax. I'm not going to sit here on pins and needles."

"Give it a rest, toots," Mr. Tea added. "Love sombreros. Cha, cha, cha."

Terry put her head in her hands and rubbed her temples. *Leave it to us to have a bird who knows his liquors*, she thought.

The woman returned and even brought a few pots of coffee and decaf coffee. They all settled down. Terry looked at her watch. "It's almost twelve-thirty. Wow."

"I feel like I've lived an extra year in these past few hours," Coach Walker said.

They sat in silence for a bit, sipping their hot drinks and nibbling on sandwiches. Terry kept thinking about Bobby Cooper. Why would anyone hurt him?

"Any ideas, Coach, on who called you? Did the voice sound familiar?" Bruce asked, breaking the silence.

"Not a clue. The person whispered. I couldn't really say if it was a man or a woman. My first reaction was it was a woman, but I can't swear to it."

"Do you have any idea why he or she called you?" Terry asked. "What do you think the caller meant by saying Bobby got what he deserved? Guilty of what?" She learned a few months ago when a former owner of her house had tried to kill her that grudges can be carried for a long time. She wondered if this was a grudge or something new.

Terry heard people walking down the hall, chatting. A knock sounded, and Bruce went to answer the door. It was Greg.

"Okay, folks. Ladies, you can go home. Mr. Wilson and Coach Walker, we have just a few more questions and then you can go home, too. Everyone has been told not to leave town. We have more to go over tomorrow. It's late and everyone is exhausted."

"Bobby's wife?" Terry asked. She felt really bad for her.

"She's staying in town at her in-laws. She's pretty shaken up."

"Okay, let's just get this over with," Coach Walker said. "Do I owe anything to the hotel for what we ate and drank?"

"Naw," said Greg. "The manager is so flustered by all of this, he says what anyone ate or drank tonight is free."

Terry looked at Shannon and Karen. "Shannon, you have your car, right?"

"Yeah, I'll drive home. Grab the bird."

"Sex on the beach," said the bird.

"No more alcohol for you, buddy," Greg said. "You're cut off."

"Jerk," squawked the bird.

"Yeah, I know," Greg said, giving Terry a smile.

Terry hung back as the others walked down the hall. "Are you okay?" she asked.

"I dunno," Greg said. "Bobby and I were friends all through high school. Seeing him with his head bashed in, floating in that pool was hard, really hard."

"Do you have any ideas?" Terry asked.

"He was whacked from behind by a baseball bat. We have to get it printed."

"What about the call Coach Walker got?"

"That's the part that scares me. Assuming he's telling the truth, and his timeline is correct, the call had to have been made almost immediately after Bobby was killed. I'm too tired to try and put it all together now."

He drew her into him and kissed her. "I'll call you tomorrow. Dream of me," he said.

She knew she would.

CHAPTER 3

Terry swore she'd just fallen asleep when the alarm went off. She whacked at it and opened her eyes to check the time. It really was seven o'clock. Ugh. Her cell phone rang and she looked at the ID. Shannon. "Yeah, I'm up. I'm so exhausted. Are you sure we shouldn't cancel tonight?"

"We already paid for the room. A number of people are booked in the hotel overnight. I was surprised at the number of people who actually booked rooms for the weekend. They wanted time to hang with friends. I'm going to go ahead. The only person who chose not to stay at the hotel was Shantel, and that's certainly understandable."

"Do you have any ideas as to who would want Bobby dead?" Terry asked.

"Not even the tiniest clue. Tom called to check on me. I asked if they had any ideas and Tom said not a one. They're hoping the baseball bat they found will have some fingerprints. I guess they're going to show pictures of the bat around. I think there were some initials carved on it. I should know, but I was exhausted."

"Well, can you call Karen's cell? I don't hear her and I don't want to have to wake her up. She scares me."

"Yeah, sure, make me do the dirty work," Shannon said, laughing.

Terry dressed in jeans, a short-sleeve shirt, and put a sweatshirt over the shirt. After turning on the coffee pot, she trudged out to the garage to start putting the boxes of decorations into the car. She stared at the decorations for a moment, remembering the hours she and Bobby had spent decorating the gym in high school. He was such a nice guy. Granted, he hung out with Chris Sanders who was the biggest egotistical jerk on the face of the Earth. Karen thought about Bobby and Bruce Wilson. Bruce was a bit of a jerk too in high school. She never understood why Donna Wiggins had a crush on him. On the other hand, she wasn't the only one. The crashing of the side door made her jump.

"Sorry," Karen said. "I'm so tired, I have no coordination. I came out to ask if you wanted me to bring you some coffee."

"Yeah, please. I was just thinking back. I was thinking about Bobby hanging out with Bruce and Chris. Bobby was so unlike them. They were pretty full of themselves, but Bobby was down to earth."

"Well, Bobby was friends with other people, like Greg. He grew up with Bruce; their fathers were friends. Chris Miller just kinda latched on to them when he moved here our sophomore year. You're right, though. Chris was one cocky S.O.B.," Karen said.

"Remember, there was that rumor our senior year that he was accused of raping someone at his old high school? Was that ever proven?" Terry asked.

"No. I'm pretty sure, and you can ask Shannon, but I swear it was not true. I heard some girl accused him, and then recanted. I could be wrong. Look, we gotta go. Let me grab the coffee. Pull the car out. Shannon should be here any second."

***

As they entered the hotel, Terry felt it still held an eerie, somber feeling. A pall seemed to hang in the air. Karen and Shannon helped her carry the boxes to the ballroom. "The pool is still cordoned off," Terry said. "I wonder if it still will be that way tonight."

"Well, I don't mean to be gross," Shannon said, "but Bobby was dead and floating in the pool. I'm sure they need to do something special, besides draining it, to have it safe to swim in again. I shudder just thinking of it."

"Well, change of subject," Karen said. "It was nice of the hotel to let us keep the decorations here during the day. It would have been a problem to try and get them here and run the teahouse this afternoon."

"Yeah, it was much easier to have the decorations already here for people like Rachelle and Sandy to put up," Shannon said, setting her box down in the corner of the ballroom.

"I knew Rachelle in high school, but I knew Donna better. I really liked talking to Rachelle last night. I imagine this is hard for her," Terry said, as she lay down on the floor. "I'm so exhausted. I could sleep right here."

"Well, you can't sleep now; we have five more boxes to bring in. You really outdid yourself, and you're gonna help bring in every last decoration, Miss Overachiever!" Karen said, prodding Terry with her foot.

As she carried in the last box, Terry looked in the dining room where they served the free breakfast. Bruce was there, and he looked terrible. Catching up with Karen, she said, "Hey, I just saw Bruce and he looks God awful. Let's stop on the way out. He's in the dining room."

After putting their boxes down, the three of them trudged to the dining room and peered in. Bruce looked far worse than Terry thought he did when she first walked by. He was wearing a t-shirt and sweatpants, his hair had not been combed, dark circles surrounded his eyes, and he had beard stubble on his face. No one else from the reunion was around. Karen surprised Terry by taking the lead. She sat at the table where Bruce was and put her hand over his. "Hey, Bruce, are you okay?"

Bruce stared at her with a blank look on his face. Terry wondered if he even recognized Karen. He said nothing.

"Bruce?" Karen asked. "Bruce, are you okay?"

"I...I...guess. The angel of death came in my room and told me Bobby got what he deserved and Chris and I were next."

"What?" Karen, Terry and Shannon said in unison.

Bruce frowned at them. He seemed to wonder why they were confused about the angel of death.

"Bruce, can we get you anything? Do you want us to call someone for you?" Shannon's voice sounded a bit shaky.

"I know it sounds crazy, but I saw her. She was right there in my room...laughing at me."

"Buddy, let's walk you back to your room. It was probably a bad dream. You're fine. We're all exhausted and in shock from last night."

"No, I'm afraid to sleep. I don't want to give her the chance to get me. I tried to call Chris, but he isn't answering. I have to stay awake."

Terry's mind raced. Bruce's parents had moved to Florida, so he really had nowhere else to go. She held up her finger, stepped out into the lobby and phoned Uncle Henry.

After she explained the situation, Henry and Rose were more than willing to let Bruce stay with them. Henry agreed that Bruce had had a terrible shock, seeing Bobby dead. Terry told Henry she'd call them back after she talked to Bruce.

Going back in the dining room, Terry whispered her idea to Karen. Karen smiled and squeezed Bruce's hand. "Hey, Bruce, let's get some clothes for you and you can go to my aunt's and uncle's house. I know you must remember Henry. He was always at your games, cheering away."

"You think I'll be safe there?" Bruce asked, sounding hopeful.

"Yes, if anyone can keep that angel of death at bay, it's them," Karen said, with a smile. "Trust me, if she shows up, Rose will yak her ear off and she'll flee."

Bruce gave a weak smile. "I'm worried about Chris. What if she already got to him? I want to warn him."

"Let's find out what room he's in and we'll stop by. Okay?" Shannon chimed in.

"I'll tell you what," Terry said. "I'll find out the room number. You guys go get Bruce's clothes."

"Okay, come to my room. I'll get my stuff," Bruce said, almost staggering from exhaustion.

Terry walked over to the front desk. "I'm with the reunion committee. Can you tell me what room Chris Miller is in? He isn't answering his cell phone. We need to get in touch with him."

The woman behind the desk glared at her. "We can't give that information out. It's against our policy."

Terry understood, but annoyance crept into her voice. "Look, we all had a rough night last night. He was a friend of the man who died; all we want to do is check on him, that's all."

A man she recognized as the manager walked up behind the woman. "Ah, yes, Ms. Sutter. You decorated the rooms for the festivities yesterday. It's okay, Ella. She's fine. Who are you looking for?"

"Chris Miller."

He looked at the computer screen and pressed a few buttons. "That would be room 576," he said, nodding toward the elevator. She turned and saw Karen and

Shannon leading Bruce into the lobby. She ran over to them. "C'mon; it's Room 576."

They rode the elevator in silence. Bruce was so nervous, he was shaking. He pushed past them as the elevator doors opened. Looking around, he took off in the direction of Chris's room. He stopped in front of a door and started to hammer at it. Other doors opened. Maids already on duty stopped in the hall to stare. Terry wanted to crawl up in a ball and die.

Chris opened the door. He looked as bad as Bruce. Actually, he looked worse, if that was possible. "Chris, you okay?" Bruce yelped, pushing the door open and shaking Chris.

Confused, Chris mumbled, "Yeah, yeah, I guess. Groggy, but okay. Why?"

Karen jumped in before Bruce could babble his nonsense. "Bruce was worried about your state of mind because of Bobby. He wanted to make sure you weathered the night okay."

"Oh, yeah. I'm still hung over, but I'll be okay." Chris gave Bruce's back a thump. "Thanks, buddy. See you later."

"Okay, now we know Chris is fine. Let's get you to my aunt's and uncle's house. You can get some rest. No offense, but you look like you need sleep," Karen said.

Bruce shrugged. "Yeah, yeah, I guess I do. Lead on. I really appreciate this. I really do. I know it sounds crazy, but I know what I saw."

Terry didn't know what to say. She was really hoping this would not be another run-in with a ghost especially an angel of death. *Wait'll Greg gets a load of this!* she thought.

***

Thankfully, Bruce remembered Henry. Terry forgot that Henry used to play poker with Bruce's dad. Rose was on the phone when they arrived at the house. It was

Henry who swooped in like a mother hen. "Ahhh, Bruce, good to see you. Good to see you," he said, pumping Bruce's hand. "Boy, I sure do miss seeing your dad every other week. I heard through the grapevine he's enjoying Florida. Fixing up some old cars, I hear."

"Yes, sir. He has an old Triumph that he's working on. I can't remember the year, but I have some photos on my phone. He's really enjoying it." Bruce's voice was flat, almost mechanic. Terry could tell by the concerned look on Henry's face that Bruce was in good hands.

"C'mon upstairs. We have a nice extra bedroom where you can get some rest, my friend. What a terrible shock to lose Bobby like that. Just terrible."

"Yes, sir," Bruce said, as he and his suitcase went up the stairs behind Henry.

As they disappeared at the top of the stairs, Rose hung up the phone and came trotting over. "Well, you will just not believe this!" Rose said, with a pleased as punch glint in her eye. Terry knew Rosie had some scoop. "I just hung up with Maude Despard; she's living in that little assisted living apartment at Fair Meadows, you know. Anyway, Maude heard from Katie Smith, her next door neighbor on the left…wait, it may the right…no, it's the left, that Margie Wiggins told Katie this morning that the police went to the Wiggins house with a picture of the bat that killed Bobby. Do you know it belonged to her son, Sam, Rachelle's and Donna's father? It was taken right out of his garage." Rose took a deep breath and zoomed on. "The bat had Sam's initials, S.W., carved on the handle. Greg, apparently, saw the initials and took a chance that it might be Sam's. Well, the Wiggins are just beside themselves. Of course, who wouldn't be, it was in their garage, last anyone knew, and now it shows up at a murder scene. How awful. Now, Maude's in a tizzy. She was going to call Greg and let him know what a ridiculous idea it was that the Wiggins could be involved, but I told her—you know how I love Greg?—that it isn't Greg's fault the bat showed up at the crime scene. Maude just needs to relax and let Greg do his job. You know, I was just saying to Henry this morning—"

Karen held up her hand and cut Rose off. "Hold up there, Rose. Slow down. Were there fingerprints on it?"

Rose blinked and her mouth opened and closed, like a fish. "Rats, I forgot to ask that. It never dawned on me to ask that. Oh, dear. Do you want me to call her back?"

"No!" Shannon, Terry, and Karen yelled in unison.

"I'm sure we'll hear more as the day progresses," Karen said. "Rose, you did good. You got the scoop. We'll make a sleuth out of you yet!" she added, smiling.

Just then, Henry came down the stairs. "Poor kid. I think he was asleep before I even left the room. He's just babbling about some angel he thought he saw. What did I miss, Rosey?"

"Well, I talked to Maude Despard, and she told me––"

"We gotta go," Terry said. "We've got to run the teahouse." Terry, Karen, and Shannon fled to the shelter and quiet of the teahouse.

CHAPTER 4

Terry was grateful that the teahouse was buzzing. She was so busy, she didn't have time to be tired. It felt good to have so many of the high school alumni come with their families. The teahouse seemed to be the place to gather, console, and gossip. Rumors were a dime a dozen this afternoon. Some said Bobby was shot, others said stabbed, others insisted he was hit with a baseball bat. Of course, Terry knew the baseball bat story was the most accurate, but she never said anything. She really didn't have time to stop to chat. Rose and Dottie Dindle were in the teahouse. They were floating from table to table. They knew everyone and loved being in the thick of things. Terry admitted to herself that Rose and her gossipy friends could probably get more scoops than the police. Terry smiled, remembering that Karen referred to them as the scoop patrol. Suddenly, Terry realized Mrs. Dindle was being unusually…quiet. She motioned Shannon over.

"Hey, what gives? Your mother has been up and down like a jack-in-the-box and no one seems to be hearing any funny noises." Terry always found Mrs. Dindle's flatulence problems amusing. Because Mrs. Dindle couldn't hear it, she didn't know she buzzed whenever she got up.

Shannon smiled. "I started getting the Listerine tongue strips and keeping them in my purse. One day, my mother asked for one, and she liked it. Whenever I take one out of my purse, she holds out her hand. Then I discovered that Gas-Ex makes tongue strips too. I keep them in my purse and substitute them for the Listerine strips. She doesn't know the difference, and it quiets her down. Voila, problem solved, or at least sometimes. I make sure I take out the Listerine strips before we leave the house. She sees me; asks for one; I reach in my purse and secretly give her the Gas-Ex." Shannon beamed; she was so proud of herself.

"Ahhhh, mon ami, you use your little grey cells," Terry said, tapping her head.

"Mais oui," Shannon said with a smile as she walked off.

"Terry," said Rose as she scuttled up, "I just saw Rachelle Wiggins and her mother getting out of the car. That back table is clearing out; I suggest you put them there." The bells over the door jangled, as the two women entered the teahouse.

"Well, hello, my darlings. Come right in. Terry will be happy to seat you," Rose chirped, hugging them.

Terry wanted to slap a muzzle on Rose. Terry peeked into the parlor area to see if people were waiting. Thankfully, the last group was just seated. Mr. Tea was keeping people amused, but she doubted that those waiting would be thrilled if another party was ushered in ahead of them.

"Oh, my, this is lovely," Rachelle cooed. "The artwork is amazing and so detailed. I can see the designs on the tiny teacups the mice are holding. It reminds me of...Peter Rabbit."

"I used my old Beatrix Potter books as inspiration," Terry said. She noticed out of the corner of her eye that Rachelle's mother's hands were shaking so terribly that the pockets of her dress looked like there was a dead fish flopping around in them.

Rachelle was squinting at a scene on the wall. "Is that a mouse peeking out from under the goose's wing? Oh, my goodness. This is incredible."

"I'm so pleased you like it," Terry said. "Let me show you to your seats." She took them to the table Rose had already scoped out for them. Rose and Dottie Dindle swooped right in. *No one, but no one, coddles and fusses over people like Rose,* Terry thought. It amazed her that Rose possessed a perfect knack for making hurting people feel cozy and comforted. Rachelle's mother certainly needed it. Dottie Dindle seemed to be becoming Rose's protégé. *God bless us!* Terry thought.

Fifteen minutes later, Terry was putting another set of scones in the pass-through for pick up as Karen came up to the window.

"Here's another order for the pumpkin spice scones," Karen said, handing the order slip to Terry. "Man, Mrs. Wiggins is a wreck. The woman is shaking so hard, the chair keeps rattling."

"What did she say?" Terry asked. "When was the bat taken?"

"How should I know? I'm too busy taking orders. Rosey, captain of the scoop patrol, is all over it. Ask her!"

As Terry watched Karen walk to a table with the order of scores, she glanced at Rachelle's table. Rose and Dottie were consoling, patting and nodding. *No one but Rose*, thought Terry.

The rest of the afternoon was a blur. Mr. Tea put everyone in a good mood by squawking, "Nice legs, toots. Three kings? I say we crown them! Here we come a whistling," which was followed by a wolf whistle, and the favorite, "Jingle bells," which was followed by him ringing his little bell.

"People think we trained him," Karen said, smirking.

"I was just thinking about the picture we found of the Gutherie sisters' Christmas party. Tea was right there. Maybe they trained him," Terry suggested. "I still find it hard to believe that Mr. Tea belonged to people who lived next door and were murdered."

"I guess we'll never know where he got his lines. He's one smart bird, though. I thought you were just adding another thing to our to-do list when we brought him home from Fair Meadows, but I was wrong. I've grown attached to him and he really is a draw factor. Customers love that bird!

Greg closed his eyes and took a deep, wonderful, bone-warming sip of his coffee.

"You look as crappy as I feel," Tom said.

"I feel as crappy as you look," Greg said with a sigh.

"Some days I wonder at what age we become too old for this," Tom mused.

After a moment of thought, Greg replied, "Thankfully, the vast majority of days do not include the murder of a childhood friend. I think that's what makes this worse. Murder is always ugly, but when it involves a brutal attack on an old friend, it's hard to keep emotions out of it."

"Yeah, about that, are you sure you want to work this one? I was there, but my emotions aren't involved. Other guys can do it. We can call in another state guy."

"I know, I know, but I want to work it. Seeing Bobby's head bashed in is something I can't get over. This was personal. The murderer targeted Bobby. It has to involve high school. I don't think the bat was an accident, either."

Tom sat on the corner of Greg's desk. "There were no prints on it, and the whole family is alibied."

"There's something missing."

"What?"

"That's why it's missing!"

"Do you think someone knows something and is holding back?" Tom asked.

Greg took another draw on his coffee. "No, I think someone knows something, but doesn't think it's important. No way this is random. I'm glad they're going ahead with the Fall Fling tonight. I'm hoping to find that last little piece we're missing."

Greg's cell phone went off. The tune "Little Old Lady from Pasadena" blazed forth. "Rose," Greg said, grinning. "Rose, everything okay?"

"Oh, yes, dear. Henry and I want to have a few people over tonight before you all leave for your reunion event, but I want to invite the Wiggins family and I'm concerned—"

Greg interrupted. "Not a problem, Rose. They're clear."

"Well, that's good news. Will you ask Tom for me?"

"Of course, he's right here. Hold on." Holding his hand over his cell, Greg whispered, "Get-together at Rose's and Henry's tonight, before the Fall Fling. You in?"

"I have to check with Shannon, but if it's okay with her, I'm in."

"Rose, Tom wants to check with Shannon—"

It was Rose's turn to interrupt. "Oh, I already asked her. She wanted to check with Tom."

"Well, I guess it's a go. We'll see you tonight. What time?"

"Oh, I think about six."

"We'll be there. Thanks for thinking of us. See you tonight." He hung up with a chuckle. Rose was so excited, she hung up on him.

"More time to snoop?" Tom asked.

"More time to snoop."

***

As Terry and Karen were getting ready to close, Rose came bustling up. "Guess what, my darlings?"

This can't be good, thought Terry. It usually isn't when she starts that way.

"Everyone, including the Wiggins, is coming over to my house for drinks before your reunion party tonight. Won't that be fun?" Rose even gave a clap of her hands.

"Oh, no, Rose," Terry said, exasperated. "Greg and Tom have an active police investigation going on. The Wiggins are a part of that. Greg and Tom can't have cocktails with the Wiggins, for Heaven's sake! Besides, I don't know Greg's plans."

"Oh, don't be silly," Rose said, with a flip of her hand. "I already called him. Greg said he and Tom don't have any conflict of interest. I had the foresight to call them first. The Wiggins, along with Rachelle and Russ, need a diversion. Henry checked with Bruce, and he's up for it. He's feeling so much better now. Shannon said she thought it would be fun. I told her half an hour ago. You're such a worry-wart, dear!"

Karen and Terry exchanged looks of shock. Rose calling anyone a worry-wart was a definite case of the pot calling the kettle black. She left through the kitchen door with a wave and a "Ta ta!"

"Dang, who was that woman, and what did she do with Rose?" Karen said.

"I was just wondering if she was always that bold and I just forgot," Terry added.

"Well, she can be a little overwhelming, that's true, but she's taken it to a whole new level, that's for sure. Huh, maybe she's feeling the power of being Captain Rose of the scoop patrol. A little power went to her head," Karen explained.

"Ahhh, but does she know she is the captain? I thought that was our secret," Terry said as she began to clean some dishes.

"Maybe she always knew. Maybe, just maybe, it was her top secret plan and we happened to figure it out," Karen said, frowning.

"The plot thickens. We shall never know, just like where Tea gets his lines. Some secrets are never meant to be discovered," Terry said, whispering.

"Amen. Crown the kings!" Tea squawked.

CHAPTER 5

Terry, once again, stared in the mirror. She turned to the left, then to the right, and then took a hand mirror and held it behind her so she could see the back of her head. No, she did not see any more gray hairs. Of course, there were the ugly bags under her eyes! She walked down the hall to Karen's bathroom. Karen was putting on mascara.

"Did you mean what you said about hating reunions because you're older and don't have children?" Terry asked.

"Yes." Karen sighed. "I'm afraid I did. I don't know why I still feel competitive with these people, but there is some part of me that feels like I've failed life."

Terry chewed her lip. "Do you think Shantel will ever find someone, now that she has three kids? How is she going to get by without Bobby?"

Karen turned and looked at her. "Where is this coming from?"

Terry felt the lump in her throat. She knew it was from being over-tired. She swallowed. She was afraid to speak.

"Okay, why are you this upset?"

"What if it were one of us? What if Greg gets killed? What if the relationship ends?"

Karen leaned up against the sink and studied Terry. "We were both feeling fine about ourselves until this reunion. I admit, I was having issues because of the divorce, but not this bad. These people will be gone tomorrow. Not everyone marries early. We are who we are. Wasn't it you who said yesterday that we should count our blessings because some people aren't at the reunion because they already died?"

"That's before I saw Sandra Hochberg. You should've seen the way she flirted with Greg. I'm surprised the woman didn't actually start drooling!"

"Oh, for the love of pizza!" Karen snapped. "Are you serious? I wouldn't give another thought to her. Really."

"I guess you're right," Terry said with a shrug. She walked back to her bathroom with a heavy heart. She still felt old.

***

At exactly six o'clock, Terry and Karen went out the back door to head over to Uncle Henry's and Aunt Rose's house. "Do most people actually snowblow a path through the back yard to their neighbors?" Karen asked.

"Maybe when they're family," Terry said, with a shrug. "Definitely, when the family contains someone like Aunt Rose. I remember Dad and Henry shoveling paths in the winter. Mom and Rose loved to be able to scoot out the back door to see each other. We created a path between our house and Shannon's. We were always tramping over with and without sleds. It was the same, either way. Now, as adults, who wants to be tramping? I say if Henry wants to snowblow, let 'im. Besides, now there's the stone path he built with the water garden."

"Does it strike you as odd that the second there's a murder, Rose needs to invite us all over? Isn't it too much like this summer?" Terry asked.

"Well, it's like we have our own little detective team going on, or should I say 'detective wannabes'? We do like to throw theories out."

"Hmmm, I am not sure Greg and Tom want the help. I don't think this should be an ongoing habit," Terry said. *Maybe this will push him away*, she thought. *Maybe this family will overwhelm him. Maybe I'll never find someone who can just accept us.*

Terry heard the patio door at Rose's house slide open. Even the porch was clear. "Hurry along, ladies," Henry said. "I'm lettin' the warm air out. Put some hustle in the bustle."

Karen and Terry scurried up the porch steps and into the house. Bruce was standing in the doorway between the back room and the kitchen.

"Thank you so much for seeing what a mess I was and bringing me here. Honestly, it's all a blur. I was so upset over Bobby's death that I drank way too much. The stress and the booze were not a good combination. I've already thanked your aunt and uncle for having pity on me."

"Wow, you look so much better," Karen said. "I barely recognized you in the hotel."

"Yeah, well, I'm ashamed to say that Chris Miller and I drank at the bar until last call last night. Sandy was with us. We were all in pretty sad shape by the time we parted company. I thought the booze would drown my sorrows, but it didn't."

"Ah, well," chimed in Henry, "you aren't the first person to figure that out, and you won't be the last. Chalk it up to a learning experience. I'm just glad you're doing better. Come and sit."

As Bruce came in and sat on the sofa, Terry heard the front door open and Greg's voice yelling, "Hello? Anybody home?"

"In the back," Henry called.

There was a stomping of feet and more voices. Terry guessed that the Wiggins clan had also arrived. She could hear Henry taking coats, along with all the nice-to-see-yous. Suddenly, she felt exhausted. She just wanted to excuse herself and go to bed. Greg's and Karen's reunion was turning into a draining experience.

As everyone walked in, Terry thought she sensed a tension in the room. She looked at Greg and saw that he was frowning. She knew he felt it, too. No one else seemed to notice as they took seats around the room. Henry and Rose brought out hors d'oeuvres and drinks.

As Rose headed back to the kitchen for more hors d'oeuvres, Dottie Dindle said, "Rose, let me help you!" Before Rose could protest, Dottie was up and a high-pitched whistle could be heard. The Wiggins family glanced around the room. Terry raised an eyebrow at Shannon.

"I couldn't find the Gas-Ex strips before we left," Shannon whispered. "I rummaged around my...Hey! Did you?" Terry shrugged. "Moi?"

Uncle Henry passed hors d'oeuvres around the room. "Rosie is famous for her cocktail hour delights," he said. "Please, help yourself."

As Rose and Dottie returned from the kitchen, Terry noted that Bruce was drinking soda and didn't seem to be too hungry. She felt sorry for him.

Sam Wiggins, Rachelle's father, leaned forward and said to Bruce, "I'm sorry to hear about your friend. We lost our daughter. She was a sweet girl who never hurt anybody. I understand what your loss is like."

"Thank you," Bruce said, lowering his eyes. He was clearly uncomfortable. "Bobby has triplets at home. I think our class should do something for them."

"I think that's a great idea," Greg piped in. "How weird is that? You, Bobby, and Chris were called the triplets in school. How perfect you should start a fund for Bobby's kids. I'm sure we can do that."

"Yeah." Bruce grinned. "They have two boys and a girl. They named them Bruce, Robert, and Christine." His voice caught.

"It's all so incomprehensible," Mrs. Dindle said. "I can't imagine anyone wanting to hurt any of you."

"Greg, could it be someone from the community, not connected with the reunion?" Rose asked. "Someone totally unconnected?"

"We really don't know," Greg said.

"Bobby told me he had to meet someone," Bruce said. "He wouldn't tell me who. That was why I eventually got up to look for him. I saw his wife, Shantel get up and I thought something might be wrong."

Terry looked around the room as everyone else did the same. It was clear that the killer was someone in their graduating class, or someone who knew about the reunion. Probably someone Bobby knew. Probably someone she herself knew.

"Did Bobby say what the person he went to meet wanted?" Rose asked.

"Naw, he did seem kinda spooked, but he didn't say anything about it except that it was weird."

"Weird?" Greg asked. "What does that mean? You didn't tell us that before."

"I actually forgot about it. He said it as a kinda side thing. He looked at his cell phone and said, 'That's weird.' Then he went back to eating dinner. A few minutes later, his phone vibrated. He looked at it and said he'd be right back. He needed to go see someone. Shantel and I asked who it was, but Bobby shrugged. He wouldn't say."

"So, there's no way of knowing if the first text was related to the second?" Rose interjected.

"Can't you see where the text came from?" Mrs. Dindle asked.

"The phone hasn't been found yet," Greg said.

No one spoke for a few minutes. It was clear to Terry that no one dared bring up the subject of the Wiggins's bat. Finally, it was Sam Wiggins who tackled the subject. "I wish I could tell you when the bat was taken. I have no clue, like I said this afternoon. In the past week, we had the antique car show in town. A bunch of us locals go to each other's houses afterward. I gave you all the names I could remember, but I think I would have noticed someone leaving with a bat."

"It wouldn't have mattered," Tom said. "There were no prints on it."

Sarah Wiggins suddenly burst into tears. Rose and Dottie jumped in with tissues. "I just don't understand why someone would use that bat. Why not buy one? Ours was in the corner of the garage. Why involve our family in this horrible tragedy?" Mrs. Wiggins sobbed, dabbing at her eyes.

"Why indeed," Rose said. "You can all relax. Tom and Greg are very good at what they do. They'll figure it out, I'm sure."

They all chatted a while about town news which seemed to help Sarah Wiggins cheer up. Finally, Rachelle cleared her throat. "We probably should be going fairly soon. I did put up the decorations today, and I want to make sure things are still fine. Terry did another terrific job. Before we go, I want to know where you got your amazing macaw."

"Actually, we adopted him from Fair Meadows. He was owned by a resident there. It turned out he used to belong to two sisters who lived in Shannon's house. It's a rather long story. He really is something, isn't he?"

"Was he Sylvia Nitmeyer's' bird?" Sarah Wiggins asked.

"Yes, she left him to Fair Meadows, and they didn't feel they could care for him, so we decided to take him. Did you know Mrs. Nitmeyer?"

"I thought I recognized him!" Rachelle said. "I thought I was wrong because it seemed like too much of a coincidence. She used to babysit us," Rachelle said. "We loved her. She called the bird Ladies' Man. I was crushed when she died."

"When Donna died," Sarah Wiggins said, "Sylvia was so sweet. She came over to the house almost every day for a few weeks. She would just sit with me. She seemed to understand that I just needed a quiet companion."

"The bird was the topic of conversation last night. Are you bringing him tonight?" Russ asked.

"Oh, no! He was just there to add to the atmosphere last night," Greg said, in an adamant tone.

"Awww," Tom said. "I find him so amusing. I think we should consider it."

Greg glared at Tom, and Terry wanted to giggle. "Tea is exhausted after such a busy day at the teahouse," Terry said. "I think he needs to rest. Besides, I think it might be too cold out."

"Oh, pish posh," said Shannon, her eyes twinkling. "He'll be fine, for crying out loud. He can come in the car with Tom, Karen, and me. Karen and I'll go get him. Tom, meet us out front." She grabbed a confused Karen and scooted out the patio door. Terry watched them leave and hoped Tea would be okay.

"Well, I agree with Rachelle," Greg said. "Let's get going and check on the decorations. After last night, let's hope tonight is quiet. Rose and Henry, thank you again for your hospitality. Mr. and Mrs. Wiggins, it was nice to see you again. Bruce, drive with us."

Terry wanted to burst out laughing at the speed with which Greg hustled them out the door. It was apparent he was perturbed Mr. Tea would be joining them. *It's so hard being a hottie,* Terry thought.

CHAPTER 6

As they walked in the front door of the hotel, Terry felt a stillness that was not there the night before. She wondered if anyone else felt it. Mr. Tea startled her by hopping in his cage and saying, "Bad memories."

"Want me to take the cage?" she asked Tom.

Tom gave her a mischievous grin. "Oh, no. I've got it. I want to try and find the perfect spot for him. He really livens things up. This gathering is gonna need that." Turning to Shannon, he said, "Let's go see if we can find that perfect place." Then, to Bruce, "Come help us."

"I'd be delighted," Bruce said. They took off, leaving the others behind.

Terry felt a pang of guilt as she admitted to herself that by taking the Gas-Ex out of Shannon's purse, she had virtually challenged Shannon to retaliate.

"Crap, I shudder to think what they have planned," Greg said. "Ter, you know I love Tea, but I swear that bird is out to get me."

Remembering that she wasn't supposed to know about Tea's comments the night before, Terry asked, "What makes you say that?"

Greg stared at her for a beat, and then said, "Oh, um, I guess I'm just being paranoid. Never mind."

Forcing herself not to crack a smile, Terry said, "I should say so! Not a good idea for a police officer. Paranoid of a bird! Really?"

Greg, an annoyed look on his face, said, "Trust me, I'm *not* paranoid."

Terry was about to try and argue the point when they entered the ballroom. Terry looked around and realized she needn't have worried about the decorations. Rachelle had done a perfect job getting the decorations up. Seeming to follow her train of thought, Karen said, "Rach, you always said Donna got all the artistic talent, but you definitely have an eye for decorating!"

Rachelle shook her head. "I can't take credit for any of this. Terry did the decorations. I just hung 'em up."

"No," Terry said adamantly. "The theme last night was the cruise, and tonight was the deserted island. I heard Russ say at Rose's that you bought the sand and the coconuts. You used green and yellow crepe paper to look like seaweed. I did the paintings and the trees, but I freely admit your touch gave the whole theme the perfect zing. You have an artistic eye like Donna did. That's what made her make-up for the plays so amazing. She and Adam Weaver definitely were able to take something simple and make it over-the-top."

"Absolutely," Greg added. He seemed slightly distracted as he looked around. Terry guessed he was checking out where Tom had put Tea. *Why is it,* she mused, *that our high school years and what people think of us are so important, even years after graduation?* She thought about her own nerves. Why did she care so much what these people thought? Why did they matter anymore? Most of them, she was seeing for the first time in over twenty years. What were their lives like now? How many came looking for some type of validation? She wondered if Tea could say something that would cause Greg to want to end their relationship. That was a terrifying thought! She began looking around for the bird.

It was Russ Wiggins who spotted the mischievous group. "Aaahh, what a splendid idea, putting Tea at the corner of the bar. Yes, yes, good place. People will be wandering up there just to hear what the bird has to say."

"Oh, Holy Mother," Greg grumbled, as Tom, Shannon, and Bruce came walking over to them, grinning like Alice's famous Cheshire cat.

"Great job on the decorations, Rachelle," Shannon said.

"That's exactly what we were just saying," Karen agreed.

"Maybe you should've helped with costumes and make-up, back in the day," Bruce added.

"Oh, no, let's not confuse my putting up what Terry did with the talent that Donna and Adam Weaver had. Those two were beyond amazing." She was quiet for a second and added, "It's kinda odd that two close friends like that both died in car accidents a few months apart."

"I remember thinking that when Donna died," Terry said.

"I think it gave us an unusual sort of comfort," Rachelle explained. "Knowing that Adam Weaver was there to greet Donna made her death a bit easier to bear. For the first few days after her death, I suffered from nightmares where I saw her in the cold ground, lonely and by herself. Then my mother mentioned that she liked to picture Donna with Adam, helping to design the set for a heavenly production. Maybe God let the two of them create a new flower. You know how imaginative they were. Whatever they were doing, we knew they were laughing."

Terry smiled. "They really complemented each other. They seemed to be the perfect team."

Rachelle nodded. "I don't think I'll ever really get over her death. I learned to cope with it. I think that's the best I can hope for."

Terry nodded. "I feel that way about the deaths of my parents. I guess learning to cope is the best we all hope for."

The group stopped at a large round table. "How's this look for a place to settle?" Shannon asked.

"Works for me," Russ said, pulling out a chair for Rachelle.

Terry touched Shannon's elbow and whispered into her ear, "Using Tea? Isn't that a bit low, even for you?"

"I have no idea what you're talking about," Shannon said innocently. "Why would I need to *use* Tea? You have nothing to feel guilty over, do you?" She glided away toward Tom.

As the group plunked down, Terry turned to Rachelle and asked, "Did Adam Weaver and Donna stay close after high school?"

Rachelle hesitated and then shrugged. "Donna pushed our whole family away after high school. It was like she was mad over something. We never did find out why. My mother felt she would come around. Before we could work it all out, Donna died."

Rachelle turned to talk to Karen, and Terry looked around at the people sitting at nearby tables. Terry loved to watch people, and the reunion was a perfect opportunity. There was Chris O'Brien. He was head over heels for Karen their junior year. Chris and Karen had gone to the junior prom together. Tonight, he sat with a woman, probably his wife, with short auburn hair and a body that looked like she worked out ten times a day. They were at a table with Tom Roberts and his wife. Tom had stopped to talk to Terry at the nametag table the night before. He had told Terry he and his wife had a number of parakeets. Tea fascinated them. Tom looked nothing like he did in high school. He was heavier and seemed less serious. Back then, he was the head of the debate team. He was focused about getting into a good law school. Terry assumed the fact that he was now an attorney, a very wealthy attorney, probably contributed to his jovial mood.

Terry saw Greg looking at the doorway. Greg quietly said, "Wow, I'm so glad he came. If I were him, I'd hate every last one of us."

"Who's that?" Russ asked.

"Winston Barnstead," Greg said. "He was the biggest nerd in school. We picked on him horribly. Turns out, the guy is brilliant. He designs alarm systems for houses and businesses. Celebrities hire him. They call him from all over the country. He's one of those people who're so brilliant, he never quite fits in with the rest of us jerks."

Turning her head, Terry watched as Winston and a woman, whom Terry assumed was his wife, came in and found a table. Winston looked great. He was tall, thin, bearded, and looked like he worked out. The woman was attractive, in a plain sort of way. She wore no make-up and her long hair was streaked with grey. She, too, looked like she worked out. Terry began to think it might be time to get more acquainted with the local gym. Winston pulled out a chair for the woman and she smiled at him. Terry felt herself smiling, too. The woman had the type of smile that drew people in.

Greg stood up. "I have to go eat crow. If anyone deserves an apology from me, it's him." As he walked away, Terry jumped up to follow him. If Greg was going to do that, she was going to join him and at least be moral support.

As they approached Winston's table, the man stood up and extended his hand. "Greg, it's nice to see you again."

Greg shook his hand. "Well, it's nice of you to say that, but I came over to apologize for being an ass in high school. We treated you very, very badly, and I have to apologize."

Winston actually laughed. "It's okay. Really. A lot of time has passed. I can't say I don't have bad memories of those days, but I have come to understand that I'm different. My friends are different, as well. We don't fit in with what is considered normal on the bell curve. We never will, really. Our brains are wired differently." He shrugged and gestured to the woman. "Greg, this is my wife, Anna."

Greg shook her hand and said, "It's so nice to meet you, Anna." Turning in Terry's direction, he said, "Winston, you might remember Terry Sutter. She was a few years behind us. She's my girlfriend."

Winston took her hand and bowed. "Of course, I remember Terry. She was one of the few girls who would actually dance with me," he said.

Terry was completely shocked; she had no recollections of ever dancing with him. Actually, she admitted to herself, she held no recollections of dancing with anyone back then. It touched her heart that Winston remembered that. It never ceased to amaze her how far a small act of kindness could go.

"You're welcome to join us for bit, if you like," Anna's quiet voice said. "I would like to know more about Winston's high school years. I met him in college. It took me years to pry him out from behind his books," she said with a smile. Terry liked her instantly.

"Well, at least you were smart enough to see his potential," Greg said.

"Anna's IQ is even higher than mine," Winston said, beaming. "She's quite smart, indeed. I'm fortunate she even noticed me."

"What made you notice him?" Terry asked, sincerely interested in finding out what drew this quiet woman to Winston, who was also very quiet.

"He was so very intense in every lab we had," she explained. "I never saw anyone as focused as I was. I felt we might be kindred spirits. When I discovered that he liked scuba diving and mountain climbing like I did, I knew I had to get to know him. One Saturday, on an outing with the scuba club, I summed up my courage, sat down next to him, and just started talking to him." She laughed out loud with the memory. "If you could have seen his face! He looked positively horrified."

Winston laughed. "I was. I couldn't believe that this girl was talking to *me*. I kept waiting for it to be some sort of cruel joke. It took me almost the whole day to realize she was sincere." Smiling, he added, "I assume Terry played a part in the decorations for this weekend. I remember her talent."

Terry felt herself blush. "I had help, trust me."

"We were sorry to hear about last night's tragedy," Anna said. "We almost didn't come tonight. We weren't even sure if tonight would be cancelled. Finally, we decided that we'd come, and if it was cancelled, we'd go out for dinner."

"I saw on the news last night that you're one of the policemen involved," Winston said to Greg.

Greg nodded. "Yeah, technically, I work for the state, but I work out of this precinct. I'm assigned to anything major."

Winston reached in his jacket pocket, took out a business card and handed it to Greg. "This hotel is one of my accounts. If you have any questions about security, please just ask. I admit I didn't have fond memories of Bobby, but he seems to have turned out okay. No one deserves to be murdered."

"Winston." Terry heard Bruce's voice behind her. Winston stood and extended his hand to Bruce. "Bruce," Winston said.

Terry noticed Winston didn't seem as pleased to see Bruce as he was Greg.

"I wanted to come over and say hello. I have a security company, and we use some of the systems you designed. You're definitely brilliant, man," Bruce said.

Winston gave a short nod. "I like what I do. The business has been good to me."

"Winston, this is Tom O'Hara, he's a friend of Greg's and mine," Bruce continued. "I wanted to introduce you. Tom was saying he's seen a few of your systems. He's impressed too."

Before Winston could respond, there was a tapping sound on the microphone. Chis Miller was standing at the DJ's table. "Hello, hello?" Chris said into the mike.

"Yakety yak," squawked Tea. Everyone laughed. "Three French hens. Nice legs, toots." Tea was hopping about his cage. He stopped and gave a wolf whistle.

Chris shot an annoyed look at Tea and said, "Ladies and gentlemen," but Tea was not finished.

"Three kings have three French hens. Bottoms-up. Sex on the beach. Greg's a hottie. Pucker up, buttercup!"

There was clapping and cheering. Calls of "Mullins, even the bird thinks you're hot," were heard about the room. Greg swore under his breath.

Chris held up his hand, and things quieted down. "Really, ladies and gentlemen, and hotties," Chris added with a smirk, bringing more laughter, "it's so nice to see everyone here tonight. I'm sure I speak for everyone when I say that the decorations in this room are astounding. Right?"

Everyone applauded and Terry felt a mix of pride and guilt. Yes, she did do the decorations, but Rachelle deserved credit too.

"I know we all needed tonight. We need to be with each other. Terry, and the reunion committee, I thank you all for making this happen." His voice caught. "Why don't you all come on up here? C'mon, c'mon," he said, beckoning.

Greg took Terry's hand and pulled her to the front. Shannon, Karen, Rachelle, and about twelve others were there.

"Let's give them all a round of applause," Chris said. As the applause died down, he said, "Tonight is our last night together. Let's make the most of it." He held up his glass. "Here's to getting lucky with some of our favorite women from high school." He laughed at his own joke, and didn't seem to notice that many people weren't laughing and were looking a bit uncomfortable over the remark. "Now, at least, we're all of legal drinking age. No more turning our headlights out as we coast down by the water, hoping the police don't see us. Those were fun, wine-filled nights. Here's to reliving a few." He set down the mike and went to join Sandy at the bar.

As Terry and Greg sat back down at the table, Tom and Bruce came back to join the group.

Shannon said, "It looks like Sandy is making some headway with Chris. I saw her polish off at least two drinks since they sat down. If that bra pushed up anything more, you wouldn't be able to see her neck. If those things bust lose, someone could get hurt. I don't think I've seen Chris look at her face once. He really is...just like he was in high school."

"Yeah, but now we're a lot older," Bruce chimed in. "Don't misunderstand me, he's my friend, but he's kinda stuck in high school. He's like this party-hearty, good-time-Charlie."

Bryan Adams's "Straight from the Heart" began playing. Terry giggled and pointed to Mr. Tea who was rocking to the music in his cage. "You give love a bad name," squawked Tea.

"What a clown," Tom said, shaking his head.

At that moment, the lights went out. There was a scream and a crash. "Don't rock the boat, baby," said a clearly agitated Tea.

"Tea!" Terry yelled, her heart pounding. The room was pitch black. Terry tried to peer through the darkness to see if Mr. Tea was okay. *I should have gone with my instincts and left him home*, she thought.

Cell phones came out as people attempted to create light. It only gave things a momentary haze. Terry caught a glimpse of the female bartender trying to keep Tea's cage from falling, but it toppled to the floor with a crash.

"Free bird," screeched Tea.

"Hold on, Tea! I'm coming," Terry called. She jumped up from the table and looked around, trying to get her bearings.

"Everyone, please remain calm and stand still!" screamed the bartender above the ruckus.

"Yes, please, for God's sake, stand still. Tea's cage fell!" Terry yelled, near hysteria. Greg put his arm around her. Tom and Greg, cell phones out, were scanning the room.

"Amen, where's the hottie?" asked Tea.

"Son of a—"mumbled Greg.

The sound of one of the large doors being opened was heard. "Ladies and gentlemen, the lights have gone out throughout the hotel. Management is working on the problem. Please stay seated to avoid injury," said a voice Terry didn't recognize. Terry could see the door was open and someone held a cell phone, but she couldn't make out a face.

"Man down. Bird overboard," Tea squawked.

"Where are the backup lights?" a man yelled. Terry was pretty sure it was Winston's voice.

Four hotel employees came through the side door with flashlights. "Remain calm and follow—"

The man didn't get a chance to finish. A scream came from the direction of the bar. All flashlights swung in that direction. The bartender was holding her cell phone and looking down. Sandy was on the ground with a small pool of blood forming around her head. Tea was standing calmly on her stomach. "Heartache tonight," squawked the bird.

CHAPTER 7

Terry stood in the cellphone lit ballroom. She couldn't erase the mental image of Sandy's crumpled body lying on the floor, blood seeping from her head. Greg and Tom were the first to reach her. Tom grabbed Tea's cage as Greg put out his arm for Tea to jump on. After Tea jumped into his cage, Greg quickly moved to take Sandy's pulse.

"Call an ambulance," he yelled over his shoulder. "Her pulse is strong, but she's losing a lot of blood."

Chaos began to break out. Terry lost sight of Tom and Greg because people, instead of staying put like they were asked, began to push and shove to get out the door. People fell and began screaming, which caused more of an uproar. Before long, there was a need for more ambulances. Tom used his muscular bulk to barge his way over to Terry. The whole group at the table was standing, waiting. Tom cautioned, "If you guys move, you might wind up as another casualty. Why the heck people don't listen is beyond me. They made things much worse by rushing for the door. We can't even see because the guys with the flashlights just got shoved back out." Muttering under his breath, Tom made his way back to Greg.

Now, about thirty minutes later, Terry sat alongside the rest of the women from their group. Karen, in a foul mood from being kicked in the shins, was on Terry's right. Next to Karen was Rachelle. A bit claustrophobic, Rachelle was trying to calm down from being enveloped by the mob. Shannon sat quietly to

Terry's left, grousing about people being idiots. Bruce and Russ stood in front of them, blocking others from stepping on them.

Sitting in the dark hotel hallway, Terry watched people, holding cell phones out in front of them, stumbled along, complaining about the hotel not having back-up lights. More police arrived and were trying to calm the panicked. The few flashlights the hotel did have, along with those that came with the police, were being used to guide ambulance crews to the injured. Sandy, still unconscious, was the first to get help. *I've had bad weekends*, Terry thought, *but nothing comes close to this.*

"Pooped bird. Crash bang. Hottie to the rescue," Tea squawked.

Shannon giggled and looked over at Tea. "Next time, if there is a next time, remind me not to be on the reunion committee. I can't get over this mess. Bobbie is killed. Sandy got hurt. And if that wasn't enough, the lights went out in Georgia," she quipped.

"Maine," corrected Tea.

"Do you think tonight can be salvaged?" Terry asked.

"I doubt it. I think lots of people left already," Shannon said.

"There you are," Terry heard Greg's voice. He and Tom apparently had commandeered a flashlight. "Word is something happened to the main circuit. It's gonna be hours. Can we go, or do we need to wait, Shannon?"

As if on cue, Terry saw the hotel manager approaching. "Ahhh, I've been looking for someone from your group I recognized. This is such a mess." His hands waved as he spoke. His shirt was untucked, and his thinning hair was askew. "We'll have to settle up later. I'll be in touch. Feel free to leave. How awful," he said, moving on.

Terry watched him flutter away. He was such a nervous Nelly.

"Is it just me?" Russ asked. "Or does that man bear a striking resemblance to Alice's white rabbit?"

Tom laughed out loud. "Now that you mention it, yeah. All he needs is the pocket watch."

"Exit stage left," squawked Tea.

As Terry and the rest of the crew tramped up the driveway toward the house, Uncle Henry opened the front door. "I thought I heard car doors," he said. "Rosie, the kids are here. No need to call," he hollered over his shoulder. Turning back to them, he said, "Hurry up, kiddos, we just saw a teaser on the news about the lights going out. Everyone else is still here. Glad to see you thought to bring Bruce, Russ and Rachelle. Might as well come in and tell the story. This way, you get to tell it once to the group. Rosie and friends will disseminate it through the town!"

"Let me just drop Tea off next door," Greg said. "He's had a rough night."

"Naw, just bring 'im in. He's family now," Henry said.

"Hot diggity! Kisses for peanuts. Pooped bird," squawked Tea, as Greg entered the house with Terry right behind him.

"I'm glad you don't mind me coming back for a while," Bruce said. "I wanted to drive my own car, but they insisted I just come along and get the car tomorrow. That hotel is starting to creep me out."

"Certainly understandable," said Henry, and he took their coats.

"Any more of Aunt Rose's yummies available?" Karen asked. "Quite frankly, I'm starving. I didn't eat many before 'cause I was looking forward to the buffet, but the hotel never got a chance to set it out. Heck, the DJ barely got started. I knew I hated reunions."

"Oh, my darlings, I am so glad you are all okay," cooed Aunt Rose, as she met them in the hallway. "Of course we have food, Karen. I even put one of my frozen lasagnas in the oven. We decided we wanted to play a few rounds of Set Back, so everyone stayed."

"Set Back," said Bruce, his voice filled with excitement. "I love that game! I used to belong to a league, but I had to give it up because of my schedule."

"Well, then, come sit down and let us beat the pants off of you," Mrs. Dindle said calmly.

"Mother!" Shannon gasped.

"Hey, your mother's a shark!" Sam Wiggins said.

"Absolutely," agreed Rose. "That woman has balls of steel."

Karen and Terry looked at each other, mouths agape. "Balls?" whispered Karen. "Did I just hear the word 'balls' come out of the primrose? I think I feel faint."

"Uh, I gotta put this cage down." Greg said.

"Oh, oh, sure," Uncle Henry said. "Terry, help Greg put it on the table in the living room. Just clear anything off of it."

Terry and Greg went into the living room with its beautiful cream carpet and blue and yellow furniture. As Greg set Tea's cage on the table, Terry flopped in one of the recliners. "I'm exhausted. I can't believe this weekend. If things weren't bad enough, Rose uttered the phrase 'balls of steel' and my head is spinning."

Greg laughed. "Yeah, I think Tea even flapped his wings at that one. I really think there's more to Aunt Rose and Dottie Dindle than we know. I think that about my mother and grandmother all the time. There's a side the kids and public see, and then there's a secret side. I swear they all have it. We caught a glimpse of it just now. Notice the Wiggins didn't even flinch. It's a conspiracy, I'm tellin' ya."

Terry rubbed her eyes and giggled. "I do believe you are on to something, Detective." She stood up and put her arms around his neck and snuggled into him. "Your powers of keen observation amaze me."

Greg kissed the top of her head. Terry felt relief. Greg loved her, she could feel it.

"Not in front of the bird," Terry whispered. She heard a flutter and saw Tea put his head under his wing. She and Greg laughed and headed back to the group. Tables and chairs were obviously rearranged as card tables, and Henry was setting up another chair. "Couples can't be partners," Mrs. Wiggins said. "Otherwise, Sam and I might wind up divorced by the end of the night. Sit at separate tables."

Terry and Greg obliged. Terry noticed Greg headed straight for Tom's table. She thought that would give him an unfair advantage, but she wasn't going to complain.

"Oh, absolutely not!" Rose barked. "No one deals one card until I find out what happened tonight!"

"Now, Rosie, maybe they don't want to talk about it," Uncle Henry said.

"It's really okay," Karen said. "There actually isn't much to tell."

"She's right," Shannon agreed. "Most people had just gotten there. We were finding tables and talking. The DJ just started to play, and the lights went out. People pulled out cell phones, and the hotel sent people with flashlights. The hotel manager said it would be hours until the lights were on. We left. That was that."

"People were ridiculous," Rachelle said. "Instead of staying put like they were asked, they rushed for the door. It was sheer chaos."

"Poor Tea was knocked off the bar. His cage opened and he flew out," Terry said. "I was scared to death."

"I can imagine," Rose commiserated.

"There were ambulances on the news," Dottie Dindle added.

"Yeah," Greg said. "A few people fell down stairs, a few were knocked down by the crowd and one of our classmates, Sandy Hochberg, who had obviously been drinking, fell off the bar stool and hit her head. Nothing that was really a big deal. The hotel is going to have an issue because their backup system didn't go on. Other than that, zip."

"Speaking of Sandy," Rachelle added, "did Chris go with her in the ambulance? The two of them looked pretty cozy at that bar. I really didn't see much after the lights went out. "

"He may have, but I highly doubt it," Bruce said. "She was feeding his need to return to being the heartthrob of high school. She lost weight and looks great now, so she enjoyed the attention she didn't get from him in high school. It wouldn't have lasted longer than tomorrow morning. Trust me. I know Chris. That poor woman was headed for heartache."

"Tell us how you really feel." Tom chuckled.

"Sorry, I just know him. Like I said, he, Bobby, and I are still friends. Bobby and I were just saying last week that he needs to move on. He has his good points, and he loves Bobby's kids, but the guy has ego issues."

"Well, we all probably contributed to that in high school," Shannon said. "Most girls had at least a short crush on him."

"Not me!" Terry and Karen said in unison.

"I said 'most'," Shannon responded. "I admit I had one. It lasted exactly three weeks. "He asked me to dance at one of the flings, and I followed him around like a puppy after that. One day, he told me that just because he asked me to dance didn't mean he wanted a groupie. I hated him after that."

"That would be him," Bruce said. "I have many bad memories of things he did. The weird thing is that he wasn't that way in private. When he hung out with us, he was normal. Get him in public, and especially around Coach, and he became a first class jerk."

"Hey, now that I think about it, Coach was around when he said it," Shannon said. "I remember it because it made it more embarrassing."

"Coach had that effect on a number of people," Greg said. "I always did exactly what he wanted in practice, but I was not one of his favorites. I didn't hang on his every word, or obey his every command. I did what he told me on the field, but I didn't go get him coffee and stuff like that."

"You were smart," Bruce added. "I wish I'd kept my distance. Chris using the word 'groupie' is kind of ironic, given the fact that Coach is a man who collects groupies. If anything, Coach may be the reason Chris is the way he is. Coach was like a father to him. His father wasn't around much, and Chris idolized Coach." Bruce shook his head. "I came this weekend for Bobby. He talked me into it. Isn't that a kick?"

No one spoke for a moment, then Russ broke the silence. "I guess Coach is a type of ring leader. He's probably a bully at heart. He targets kids and it works 'cause he's a coach."

"That pretty much sums it up," Greg said. His cell went off and he looked at it. He rolled his eyes at Tom. Terry knew that meant it was work.

"Mullins. What? Are you sure? How do you...Yeah, okay. We're on our way." He flipped the phone shut.

"And?" Tom asked.

Terry noticed Greg was pale. Her heart skipped a beat. This had to be bad. "They just found Chris. He's dead. Someone shot him. He was dumped on Coach's lawn."

A collective gasp went up from the group.

"What do you mean, he's dead?" Bruce bellowed.

Terry noticed Greg was clearly rattled. "I only know what they told me. I...I... am so sorry, Bruce. I can't believe it myself. How could this possibly happen?" Greg whispered. "There were cops all over the place within ten minutes of the lights going out."

CHAPTER 8

Greg looked at Bruce, whose face went completely pale. *No way he was expecting this,* Greg thought.

"Holy mother of pearl," Henry said, with a whistle. He looked directly at Bruce. "You okay, son?"

Bruce stared blankly at him and mumbled, "No, no, not really."

Everyone was too shocked to speak. Tom regained his composure and was up and heading toward the front hall. "We can get our coats, Henry. Just hold down the fort."

All eyes stared questioningly at Greg. "Yeah, what he said," Greg said. "I can't even get my head around this. Bruce, you need to stay here, if that's okay, Henry. He isn't safe at the hotel."

"Of course, of course," Henry said. "Just go!"

Greg followed Tom, grabbed his coat and was going out the front door when he heard Tea squawk, "Tangled webs, tangled webs."

"You want me to drive?" Tom asked. "You look rattled. You okay?"

"Yes, I want you to drive, and I don't know how I am. How the heck did Chris wind up dead on Coach's lawn? You and I were up front pretty quickly. We stayed with Sandy until the ambulance got there. Did you see Chris during that time?"

"No, but I was more focused on the crowd of people pushing and shoving. It was really too dark to make out many faces. Maybe we'll find some clues as to what happened when we get there," Tom said.

Coach's house was only ten minutes away. As they pulled up, Greg could already tell that no one else but the guys who took the call were there. They were obviously having a hard time calming Coach. As he opened his door, Greg heard Coach yelling obscenities. Greg slammed the door and sprinted up the driveway. "I got this," he said to the other officers. They looked grateful and scurried over to Tom, who was looking at Chris's body on the front lawn. Greg saw Chris's head with a bullet hole in the forehead. Greg swallowed the bile rising in his throat and continued toward Coach. Greg knew he couldn't think about Chris now. There would be time for that later.

"Coach, you gotta calm down. Look at me," Greg said, gently placing both his hands on the man's shoulders. Coach was weaving slightly. His eyes had a slight glaze.

Coach shrugged him off. "How could you let this happen? Where were you lazy idiots when this happened to him? I pay taxes for your salaries and this is what happens? What's wrong with this town?" Coach followed with a string of words that insinuated that Greg had sex with his mother and that his mother was unwed when she had him.

Enough was enough. Greg knew he needed to get Coach to focus and tell them what happened. Greg grabbed Coach's shoulders and got in his face. "Shut your big, fat mouth!" he screamed. "Shut your mouth before someone shuts it for you. Acting this way helps nothing! Either shut up and tell me what happened, or take your yap inside!"

Coach looked completely stunned for a second, then sat down on the front step. Greg wondered if it was because of what he'd said, or if it was the booze Greg smelled when he'd gotten up close and personal.

"I don't really know what happened. I was asleep on the couch. I heard a loud bang; it sounded like a gun shot, which it obviously was, and when I opened my door, there he was. I ran outside, but it was too late. He was lying there with the bullet hole in his head. Someone must have called the police 'cause I don't remember anything until...I guess until those guys," he gestured to the two officers with Tom, "came and pulled me off him."

"Do you remember any other noise besides the gun shot? Something like a car? Voices? Anything?"

Coach sat still, his eyes closed, thinking; his body still weaving. "Yeah, I heard a car drive off just after the bang, which I guess was the gun shot. Like I said, I was sleeping. It took me a minute to get my bearings."

Greg suspected that Coach was passed out drunk on the couch, and not really sleeping when all this occurred. Had the killer counted on that? Why hadn't Chris shouted out or protested before he was shot? Was he unconscious? "Don't move," Greg told Coach. Greg went over to Tom and Officers Burdick and Taylor. "What do you have?"

The other two deferred to Tom. "It looks like he was shot here. I imagine we'll find the bullet in the ground. This black set of wings was by him."

"Black set of wings?" Greg interjected. "Didn't Bruce mention something about black wings?"

"Yeah, I was thinkin' that," Tom agreed. "I'll request they be dusted for any prints, but we need to ask Coach about them. Coach may have thrown the wings to the side. When Burdick and Taylor arrived, Coach was slumped over him, crying."

"Yeah, Coach said he didn't call it in. Do we know who did?"

"Not really," Officer Burdick answered. "We got a call from dispatch that said someone reported a dead body at this address. You'll have to call dispatch. I think Marge is on duty. She took the call."

Greg grabbed his radio and told Marge to call his cell. It rang about ten seconds later. Greg looked at the caller ID. "Marge, I need to know who called in the dead body on Winslow Street," he said.

"Actually, it was kinda weird," she said. "I took one call that said the body of a dead skunk was left at the address, and the caller hung up. That caller was a woman. Then one of the neighbors called and said he'd heard a gunshot and something seemed wrong. The man said he lived across the street, and his neighbor seemed to be screaming over a body on the front lawn. He gave his name as Lester Piper at 317 Winslow Street."

"You say the first call reported a dead skunk?"

"Yeah, that was a woman. She sounded like she was laughing. Want me to play it back for you?"

"Not right now. I'll get it later. Anything else you can think of?"

"Well, the caller about the skunk was not alone. I could hear other voices laughing in the background. It sounded like they were in a car."

"Okay, we'll be in later to hear it. Thanks, Marge." Greg hung up and stared up at the sky. He thought about the black wings, the phone call about the skunk, and he thought about high school and who they'd all been. It all swirled like fog in his head. He pictured the football team during practice. They were a close group and worked well together. Snapshots of them hanging out together floated through his head.

"Well?" Tom asked. His voice snapped Greg back into the present.

"Well, I've gotta call the State barracks. This is getting bigger and bigger. First, given the black wings by the body, I'd lay money that Bruce didn't hallucinate last night. I don't know exactly what happened, but he saw something, someone, real. Secondly, we gotta go to the hospital and talk to Sandy. We have to know exactly what was going on when the lights went out."

CHAPTER 9

Just after Greg left, Terry sat down next to Bruce. She didn't know what to say, but she figured she could at least sit by him. Karen got up and went into the kitchen. Terry heard her open the fridge. She knew Karen was pouring herself, and probably Shannon, a large margarita. It was Tea who broke the silence.

"Speak up. Speak up. Sex on the beach."

Bruce's head snapped up. He stared around the room. He cleared his throat and looked at Sam Wiggins. "I didn't want to come this weekend, but I've told you, Bobby insisted. He insisted because we needed to make things right, to put the past to rest. Chris was having nothing to do with it, he was furious, but Bobby and I were going to put it right."

Terry had no idea what Bruce was talking about, but the Wiggins seemed to. Rachelle grabbed Russ's hand, and her mother stared out the porch door. There were tears in her eyes.

"Let's not—" Rose started, but Bruce put up his hand, and Henry gave her "the death glare."

"In May of our senior year, your daughter, Donna, had a crush on Chris, a big crush. Chris took advantage of that. There was a party in Kennybunk. We were all beyond drunk. I don't know how it happened, really, but Coach held Donna down and Chris raped her. Then Coach insisted the rest of us follow suit. Then Chris held her down for Coach. Although, by that time, she was in shock. She wasn't moving."

"Oh, the poor girl," Terry said, her voice catching in her throat.

Bruce nodded and continued. "Coach said that—well, it doesn't matter what he said. There are no excuses. What happened was wrong and disgusting. I know this has nothing really to do with what happened this weekend, but I can't help wondering if there were others I didn't know about. Although, I think Bobby would have told me. I can't take back what we did to Donna. I imagine Donna told you, but I needed to apologize. I'm just sorry it couldn't be to her."

The silence was thick and weighed like a heavy, wet blanket. Terry felt her stomach begin to churn and her mind to reel. Sarah Wiggins was crying openly now. Rachelle looked scared, and kept glancing at Russ and her father.

Sam Wiggins shook his head. "We did know. Not everything, but enough. I wanted to wring your neck when I saw you. What you did caused Donna to shut the rest of us out. She was so ashamed that we never found out until…much later on. I've spent years wishing I could kill you with my bare hands. Now I see you're sincere. I can see it in your face that your remorse is real. I certainly can't say I feel all warm and fuzzy toward you, but I can say I feel some relief. Toward you and Bobby, that is. Not that scum of a coach."

Sarah Wiggins took a shaky breath. She snatched a tissue from the nearby box. "I've wanted nothing but to spit in your face for years."

"Why didn't you have us all thrown in jail?" Bruce asked, his voice shaky. "We certainly deserved it."

"It's a long story," Rachelle interjected. "The truth didn't come out right away. By the time it did, it seemed better to move on. We actually didn't know the whole story until right now. We knew part of it. Now

Donna's behavior makes sense. We just knew..." Her voice drifted off.

Terry wondered what really happened. What did they know? How could the Wiggins be around Bruce all weekend and act normally? That made no sense.

"Sorry doesn't feel like enough," Bruce said, his voice cracking. "Bobby and I have made donations every year to the scholarship fund you set up in Donna's name. We did it anonymously. We were afraid you wouldn't take the money, otherwise."

Terry looked around the room. Karen and Shannon downed their margaritas. Karen got up and Shannon handed her her glass. Karen always said, "When things get awkward, drink," and this was awkward.

"Mr. Sanders, I'm sure you don't want me staying here anymore, but I'll need a ride back to the hotel," Bruce said in a quiet voice that broke Terry's heart. That surprised her. She wasn't sure what she should feel. Hatred? Disgust? Pity? Should she hold this past act against him, or judge him by who he was now?

"Oh, no, you're not going anywhere," Henry said firmly. "You may have forgotten, but I have not, what brought you here in the first place. You are not, in my opinion, safe in that hotel and I insist you stay put."

"Holy cr...crackers," Karen blurted out. "I forgot about that. What the he...heck did you see yesterday? It can't be coincidence."

Bruce's eye's widened and his jaw dropped. He stared from face to face. It was clear he had no answer.

"I have to agree with Henry," Sam Wiggins added. "I may be disgusted with you at the moment, but I agree you're safer here than at the hotel. Stepping up and doing the right thing, and meaning it, is moving in the right direction. We can't change what happened, but letting you get killed as well will solve nothing."

Rose cleared her throat. "Well, I do feel that Greg and Tom need to know about this. It certainly seems possible that something similar happened to some other girl. It could all be related."

"Tangled webs, tangled webs," Tea squawked.

CHAPTER 10

"I cannot believe how totally exhausted I am," Karen said, as the sisters walked through the back yard to their home. "I think my body is on autopilot." She unlocked the back door and they entered the kitchen.

"I was exhausted hours ago," Terry said. "I've now passed that benchmark. I think I've gone totally numb." She opened the cage door and held out her arm for Tea. She felt he needed a few moments of freedom before bed.

"Shiver me timbers," Mr. Tea added. "Fire and ice. Fire and ice."

Karen lifted an eyebrow at Terry. "I'm too tired to even guess," Terry said. "C'mon, Mr. Tea. Let's get you settled, so I can go to sleep."

"Greg's a hottie," Tea squawked.

Karen burst out laughing. "Ya got that right, Tea. My sister is one lucky lady."

"Please, do not encourage him," Terry said, stroking Tea's feathers. "I've got enough on my mind without worrying about Tea embarrassing Greg."

"Are you serious? Really?" Karen barked, following her sister into the front room. "Two weeks ago, when he and Henry were fixing the dishwasher and he took off his shirt, Shannon and I almost wet ourselves, and Shannon has Tom!"

Terry collapsed on the couch with Tea on her arm and began howling with laughter. Tea was completely unphased. "Wet yourselves?"

"Oh, heck, yeah," Karen continued, now on a roll. "I grabbed a napkin to wipe the drool off my face before anyone saw it. Didn't you wonder why Shannon kept fanning herself with the junk mail? Her panties were on fire, for heaven's sake."

Terry could not stop laughing. She gasped for air. "T—T—T—Take Tea...I can't..."

Karen, with a self-satisfied smirk, reached out her arm and Tea hopped on. "Hot stuff," he remarked.

Karen opened the cage door and Tea jumped in. "Fire and ice," he squawked again.

"P—P—P—Panties on f—f—f—fire," Terry hooted, unable to regain her composure. .

"Okay, sister dear, you're giddy. Let's get you upstairs," Karen said, helping Terry to her feet.

Flopping onto the bed, Terry was still giggling. Tears ran down her face from laughing so hard. She forced herself to take slow deep breaths. She listened to the ticking of the clock as she drifted off.

She was in school again. There were too many people, and she couldn't get through to get to class. The bell had already rung, but the hall was still crowded. Terry looked at her watch. She was going to be late. She saw Bobby up ahead of her. She called out to him. He turned around, but he couldn't see her. She jumped in the air and waved her arms, but there were too many people. "Danger, danger," someone was yelling at her. She heard Karen calling to her. Terry started running, but she fell. She kept falling and falling.

"Terry!"

Terry sat bolt upright. Karen was shaking her. "Danger, danger," Tea was squawking downstairs.

"What?" Terry was still groggy. She couldn't focus.

"Something's wrong," Karen said, pulling at Terry. "C'mon, get up. The phone rang and I answered it. The woman was looking for Bruce. I asked who it was, and she hung up. Tea started squawking a few minutes later."

"Call Henry," Terry said. "Just call Henry."

"I tried, no answer."

There was the sound of smashing of glass and screeching tires. A car roared off. Terry bolted out of bed. The two sisters bounded down the stairs and out their front door.

"Holy mother of pearl!" Karen screamed. "Henry's house is on fire!"

Both girls raced toward the house, waving their arms and yelling for Henry and Rose as they went. A door slammed and seconds later, Shannon was right with them. Sirens wailed in the distance. Terry could barely breathe. She was aware that her feet were bare and she was running through snow, but she didn't care. She watched the flames burst through the upstairs window. Karen reached Henry's door first. The door flew open and Rose slammed into Karen, sending both of them toppling into the snow-covered bushes. Bruce rushed out, caught the movement in the bushes in his peripheral vision and stopped to see Rose on top of Karen. Henry, running full bore out of the house, careened into Bruce and they flew forward.

 Rose's very ample bosom was hiding Karen's head. Karen kept trying to move Rose, but at each attempt, Karen's hand disappeared and Rose screamed, "Ow!"

Karen quickly gave up and her arms stuck straight out, flapping up and down, doing no good whatsoever. From underneath Rose came a muffled scream for help.

Henry scrambled off of Bruce, ran to the bush, grabbed Aunt Rose's ankles and attempted to yank Rose off of Karen. Unfortunately, it was definitely a job for a younger man. Bruce jumped up and went to help. Henry was tugging on Rose, but she and Karen were now sunk in the bushes. Panic ensued with Terry and the Dindles yelling for fear someone would get hurt, being so close to the house. Bruce's eyes were wide. He lunged forward to grab Rose around the chest, but he backed off, his frown showing he thought better of it.

"For the love of pizza, don't stand on formalities, man," Henry bellowed.

Bruce reached around Rose and hoisted her off of Karen. He quickly pivoted and set her down. Rose wobbled. Shannon caught her and the two toppled over. Bruce grabbed Karen and picked her up in a fireman's carry and ran a few feet away from the house.

Police cars skidded to a stop in front of the house as Rose rolled off of Shannon. Terry couldn't make out who the officers were, but she knew it was not Greg and Tom. Terry turned to ask Uncle Henry if he was okay, but he wasn't there. She looked around and realized the front door was open. "Henry!" she shrieked. "Henry went back inside."

Bruce sprinted past Terry. Without thinking, she followed him through the door and right up the stairs. Henry was in the front bedroom with the fire extinguisher that was kept by the front hall closet. Bruce yanked a bedspread from the hall closet and began to try and smother the fire on the bed. Terry grabbed a bucket from under the bathroom sink, scooped up toilet water, and ran into the bedroom, throwing the water on the bed. There were thundering footsteps on the stairs and firemen burst in with fire extinguishers. In a blink, it was over. The outside wall was black, the curtains were gone, the dresser was a scorched mess, the bed was a blackened heap, but it was over.

The firemen guided them down the stairs and out the front door. Rose, Karen, and the Dindles surrounded them. Terry heard two car doors slam. Tom and Greg ran toward them. Before she could speak, she was knocked to the ground, a huge weight on top of her. Oh, God, it was Henry. Rose and Karen began screeching. Henry rolled to the right, grabbing his chest.

"Give him air," Greg yelled. The paramedics ran over to help. Terry realized they came with the fire trucks. She knew she should move, but she couldn't. Her body was frozen in fear. Greg wrapped his coat around her, and scooped her up. All she could hear was Rose calling out Henry's name. Her eyes followed the sound. Mrs. Dindle was hugging Rose as Rose clung to her. Karen, Shannon and Bruce huddled together. Tom stood behind Shannon, his hand on her shoulder.

"Terry? Terry?" Greg was whispering her name. It was all too much. She closed her eyes and tears spilled down her cheeks. She was suddenly so, so cold. Her body shook. She couldn't stop it.

"She's going into shock," Greg yelled. There were people, there were blankets. She couldn't get warm, she couldn't open her eyes. She could barely breathe. Sirens, she was hearing more sirens. Were they close? She couldn't tell. It was all just too much.

CHAPTER 11

Greg's head spun. He felt light-headed and nauseated. Rose and Mrs. Dindle were with Henry, and Shannon and Karen were with Terry. He, Tom and Bruce could only sit and wait. Tom and Bruce returned from the coffee shop across the street and handed him a coffee. As they joined him at the round table, Tom asked, "How are you holding up?"

Greg had no idea what to say, so he looked at Bruce and asked, "What in God's name happened?"

"I was in bed and I heard the phone ringing. I heard Rose answer. She came in my room and handed me the phone. She said someone was looking for me. When I answered, a male voice said, 'Enjoy Hell.' Henry came in and I told him what happened. He had his cell phone and he called 911, I guess. He was on the phone when there was a crash and fire flew in the window. Henry screamed, 'Run!' and shoved Rose in the direction of the stairs. I jumped out of bed, Henry was still yelling, 'Run, run, run! and we all ran down the stairs. It all happened so fast."

"Did you recognize the voice on the phone?" Tom asked.

"No. It didn't sound familiar. What about Chris?"

"I can't tell you anything at the moment. I have to ask that you say nothing to anyone. We were just leaving here from trying to talk to Sandy when dispatch called us." Greg saw the look of despair on Bruce's face. "The other night, when you thought you saw the angel of death, what exactly happened?"

"I woke up, and she was standing over me. I didn't know what was going on. She was all in black, with black wings. I think I asked what was going on. It's all rather fuzzy. I mean really fuzzy, like blurry. It was like I couldn't focus. She laughed and said Bobby got exactly what he deserved, and Chris and I would be seeing Bobby soon. She came toward me, and put her hand on my face. I was sure I was gonna die. The next thing I remember, it was about five in the morning. I was sure I was dreaming until I saw part of a black feather on my pillow. I got up, grabbed my wallet and ran out to the coffee shop. I figured I was safer with people. I called Chris's cell, but he didn't answer. I was pretty sure he was with Sandy. They were headed to her room when we left the bar. I was too scared to leave the coffee shop. I sat there until the girls found me."

"What did you do with the feather?" Greg asked urgently.

"I left it on the bed when I bolted out of there."

Greg looked at Tom, and Tom nodded. He got up and walked away with the cell phone to his ear.

"Can't you tell me anything about Chris? Please," Bruce begged Greg.

Greg sighed. "I think we're going to try and keep as much as we can out of the media, for now. Tom and I came here and talked to Sandy. She remembers Chris saying he felt funny. He started to fall off the barstool, and that's when the lights when out. Someone hit her over the head with something, probably a bottle, and knocked her out."

"How did Chris get to Coach's house?"

"That's the big question. We think whoever is doing this is looking for recognition, that's why we're saying as little as we can to the media. The less you say to anyone, the better. Tom is sending someone to the hotel now to look through your room."

Bruce's eyes filled with tears. "Greg, I gotta tell you something. I told everyone else after you and Tom left, last night. Something happened in high school that might somehow tie into this."

CHAPTER 12

"I'm bushed," Terry said, sitting down on one of the tearoom chairs and putting her head in her hands. "It's been such a long day and it's only five-thirty. I know I slept through most of it, but I'm still exhausted. I guess having a panic attack can do that to you. Of course, the meds they prescribed to relax me must have helped me sleep."

"Well, I didn't ever get back to sleep last night. By the time I got you home, it was six o'clock in the morning. I was still a bit shaky from you and Henry both going to the hospital. I knew if I went back to bed, I wouldn't want to get back up. Thank God for Greg's sister, Anna. She was such a help. Shannon and I were walking zombies. If I hadn't known Henry was going to be okay, I would have closed the place today. I'm so tired, but I felt we needed to let everyone come here for dinner. Rose is such a good sport about doing dinners and now she needs the support."

"It does feel odd for us to be having everyone over for dinner," Terry said. "That's Aunt Rose's department."

"Well, given that there was a fire in her upstairs bedroom last night, I thought it was the decent thing to do!" Karen said, sounding a bit snarky.

"I'm not complaining, I was just commenting. You're *cranky* tonight! Sheesh!"

"I'm sorry. I'm so glad we're closed tomorrow. I'm at my wits end. The last three days have been from the pit of Hell! Ooops, I mean *h, e*, double hockey sticks."

"Kar, do you have any idea why Chris's death hasn't been mentioned in the media? It seems sort of strange. Doesn't it?"

"Actually, I didn't even think about it. It could have something to do with notifying his family. Who knows? Oh, I'm so sorry. I forgot to tell you that Rachelle called. They decided to leave today. She wanted me to tell you thanks for everything. She and Russ just want to get home. They don't want their kids freaking out over something they see on the news."

"It was really nice to see her again. Russ is a really nice guy. I was thinking this afternoon that I never once asked to see pictures of their kids. I was so distracted. I feel like a heel."

"I wouldn't," Karen said. "She was free to whip the pictures out any time. Besides, we get Christmas cards year after year without any pictures. I don't think she really thought about it. It's probably just the way they are. No biggie. I feel bad I didn't have a chance to call Sandy's parents and ask how she is. Of course, I haven't seen her in years. The whole reunion thing is weird. If we have another one, I'm going into hiding."

"Three French hens, two turtle doves," squawked Tea

"Yes, yes, my feathered friend. Tomorrow, I'll get out the last of the Christmas decorations. I know you want Christmas," Karen said.

"String up the lights! Deck the halls! Prisoner of love," Tea added, and he rang his bell.

Karen frowned at Terry and walked into the parlor. "Prisoner of love?"

"Saint Nick," Tea said.

The front door opened and Uncle Henry came in, followed by Aunt Rose, Bruce and Greg. Rose carried a few containers. As she handed the containers to Karen, Rose began her typical babble. "Greg actually came and got us. We're staying a few nights at the hotel where the reunion was held. Our room is one of the ones with the little kitchens. It's perfectly fine for what we need. Anyway, Greg getting us saved Henry the drive. Greg is such a dear. "

Greg blushed and handed Terry a brown grocery bag. "Booze."

"Smart man," Karen chimed in. "C'mon in, everyone. Have a seat in the parlor with Tea. I cheated and ordered pizza. Rose brought hors d'oeuvres."

"I can only drink water, for now," Henry said. "No alcohol with this medication, and no caffeine. I'm not likin' life."

"Henry!" Rose barked. "We thought we lost you last night. How can you say such a thing?"

Henry sighed. "Rosey, you know I'm not a fan of water, or soda, or anything but iced tea, and various cocktails. I can't stand being treated like an invalid. There was no heart damage. I was under too much stress."

"Let me help you in the kitchen," Bruce said to Karen. The two of them zipped into the kitchen and Karen shut the pass-through doors. Terry and Karen always got nervous when Henry and Rose had their little bicker sessions. The bickering never amounted to much, but the girls hated it.

"So, Henry, have they indicated when they might reopen the pool?" Greg asked.

Yes, change of subject! Terry thought gleefully.

"No, but the hot tub section is open. The hotel even rented some large hot tubs. I know the skiers like coming back and relaxing with a swim and a soak in the hot tub. For now, the hot tubs will have to do. People with kids really like it, too. Rosey and I do like sitting poolside for cocktails, even if I am alcohol-free. The area is fixed up nicely. I imagine the hotel really had to hustle to pull it off. They have a ton of plants, a few large fish tanks and, as I said, the hot tubs. There are some trellises around with benches and large potted trees. I'm hoping the insurance company can get things moving soon on my house. I just want to get busy putting up the Christmas lights."

"Oh, for mercy's sake, Henry," Rose snapped. "It all can wait. It's you we want."

"Okay, okay. Knock it off, you'll give me tummy troubles," Karen said, walking into the room with a tray and Bruce right behind her with glasses.

"Do you hear what I hear?" Tea asked. The doorbell rang.

"Freaky," Greg said to Terry as he got up to answer the door.

The wonderful aromas of cheese, sauce, peppers, onions, garlic and oregano wafted through the front door.

"Ah, slices of heaven," Bruce said as he swooped in and paid the pizza delivery man.

"Hey! That was supposed to be our treat," Karen said.

"It's the least I can do after all you've done for me," Bruce said.

"But you've been through—"

"No arguing," Bruce broke in. "You'll give me tummy troubles."

Karen's mouth dropped open as everyone else burst out laughing.

Terry and Greg gave each other a quick glance. She knew Greg was thinking what she was thinking. *Was Bruce flirting?* Greg smirked.

Dinner was fantastic. Terry loved the pizza from Turkey Turd Lane Pizza. There was nothing like it. When she had worked in Connecticut, no one believed there was such a place. Terry had taken pictures to prove it. Despite the amazing fare, Terry felt an awkwardness at dinner. No one wanted to discuss why they were eating here. It was the proverbial elephant in the room. Even Rose had a few glasses of White Zinfandel. Karen raised her eyebrows at Terry when Rose poured herself glass number two. When dinner was finished and Rose poured number three and sashayed herself into the parlor, Bruce gave Henry a big grin. Henry just shook his head. Everyone followed behind Rose. Karen grabbed the wine and did an over-emphasized sashay into the parlor and plunked down next to Aunt Rose.

"Soooo, Aunt Rosey, anything on your mind?" Karen asked.

"Of course there is!" Rose barked. "I feel just terrible about answering that phone call last night. I should have hung up right away. I'm such a ninny!"

Greg regarded Rose for a moment. "Honestly, Rose, whoever it was already narrowed down Bruce's whereabouts to either your house or this one. There's no reason to think that he wouldn't have attacked both houses."

"He?" Bruce asked. "It was a woman on the phone."

"Well, then that woman must be a member of a softball league. The person threw a Molotov cocktail through that window from about one quarter of the way up the driveway. I saw the tracks in the snow. That person has an arm! I couldn't have pulled it off. I talked to one of the investigators today, and he said that if he hadn't seen the smashed window and the bottle, he wouldn't have believed it. A woman could have been driving the car, or even a passenger, but I would be surprised if the person who actually tossed it was a woman. It isn't impossible, but I would say it's highly unlikely."

"So, let me get this straight," Karen said. "You think a number of people are involved?"

"Look, I'm limited in what I can say. All I can say for sure is that it took more than one person to move Chris's body. According to the toxicology tests, he was drugged before he was shot. This is not random. It's well-planned revenge. I spoke to Bruce today, and he has agreed to stay at my house for a bit. You might as well know that someone trashed the heck out of his hotel room. We towed his car. It's hidden away at the moment. That's really all I'm comfortable saying. I'm sure you all understand."

Henry looked at Bruce. "You swear, I mean truly swear, you cannot think of any reason for this?"

"I swear," Bruce said, holding up his right hand. "The worst thing I ever did in high school was what we did to Donna. Bobby and I both were sick over it. Bobby told Shantel what happened before he asked her to marry him. Obviously, someone has a vendetta against the three of us, but I can't think who."

"Um, what about Winston Barnstead?" Terry asked.

"Who's that?" Rose asked.

"He's this really, and I mean *really*, smart guy from high school. Almost everyone was a total jerk to him. He was the nerdiest guy you'd ever want to meet," Karen explained.

"That's the thing," Bruce added. "Yeah, we were total jerks to him, no doubt. However, we weren't the only ones. Actually, we pretty much ignored him. We were the least of his troubles. I suppose he could still be angry, but he'd have to want to do away with most of our class."

"What about Sandy?" Karen asked. "You all made fun of her. Maybe she's out for revenge with someone else."

They all pondered that for a moment. "It's a possibility, I suppose," Greg said. "She could have drugged Chris's' drink, and then had her partner hit her over the head. Still, her partner must have a great throwing arm. Besides, Sandy seemed truly surprised and despondent over Chris when Tom and I talked to her at the hospital."

"It wasn't her voice on the phone. That, I'm sure of," Bruce said. "I spent Friday night hanging out with her and Chris. I think her voice would have clicked in my head."

"Maybe she has a team," Rose ventured. "She could have a strong lesbian lover."

"Rose," Henry said. "Really."

"Hey, some of those lesbians are quite butch," Rose said, obviously proud of herself for knowing the lingo.

"Okay, Bruce, did you see her with any woman with amazing-looking arms?" Greg asked.

"Once she glommed onto Chris, I didn't see her with any woman," Bruce said.

"Folks, I don't mean to put a damper on things, but I'm exhausted," Henry said. "Is Bruce going with you tonight, Greg?"

"That's what we planned. I think we're all exhausted. Tom and I will figure this out. Don't you worry. It must have some link to the past."

"Well," Rose said, sitting up straighter, "if it has something to do with the past, the best place to begin is Fair Meadows. We seniors can't always remember today, but we certainly remember yesterday. Someone is bound to remember some gossip from when you all were in high school!"

Terry burst out laughing. "That's quite true, Aunt Rose. Quite true. Maybe someone there would know something about the past that we don't."

CHAPTER 13

Greg's mood was as black as black gets. He yanked open the police station door and it banged against the brick wall. He wanted to hit someone, or maybe it was strangle. Nope, it was knock down and stomp on. He wanted to throw a mega adult temper tantrum. He could hear his heart pounding. He stopped, took a deep breath, set his coffee down and just stood at his desk.

"Issue?" Tom asked.

Greg held up his hand. He needed a moment to collect himself. "Just give me a sec. I'm beyond pissed off right now, and I need to calm myself down."

Tom wisely went back to work, calmly writing his reports and sipping coffee. Greg was glad Tom knew when it was best to back off. Maybe it was a guy thing. His mother and Anna usually pestered him about sharing his feelings. *All I want to share right now is my fist*, he thought.

He picked up a stack of files from his desk. Tom looked up. "You gonna file those or throw 'em?"

Greg laughed. "File. It's one of those mindless tasks that I can use to chill for a second."

Tom nodded. "Knock yourself out, killer. I gotta stack right there," he said, pointing to a group of files sitting in a wire basket.

Greg glanced at the files. "Yeah, well, don't hold your breath," he said, walking toward the file cabinet in the back.

Twenty-five minutes later, Greg came back and plunked down with a sigh. Tom regarded him carefully. "And, are we sharing yet?"

"Sure," Greg said. "Remember about three years ago when I started working out of here? I told you I was glad to be away from someone."

"Yeah, it was a guy named Alex Thumhart, as I recall."

"That would be him. Well, get this, he's going to be helping with the reunion killings!"

Tom whistled. "I guess that will be the last time you ask the State for help."

"Oh, but I didn't. I didn't have a chance. I just got a call from Greenley, telling me that Thumhart is on his way."

"Greenley, as in your boss?"

"Yup."

"Why?"

"Too much, too fast. I'm not saying the help isn't needed, but this guy is a hindrance, not a help. The last case we worked, he had a priest arrested. I tried to tell him that he was on the wrong track, but he pushed it through. I found the real killer. There were all sorts of apologies owed the priest."

Tom nodded. "I remember that. It was all over the news. The priest's fingerprints were on the murder weapon, which was the wine chalice. Right?"

"That's the one. First, it was the wrong chalice. Second, there were also a bunch of other prints. Thumhart has this ability to con the higher-ups. I don't get it, but they fall for his half-baked theories every time. Ugh! I can't stand the guy!"

As if on cue, the main door opened and in walked Alex Thumhart. Greg felt a distinct churning in his stomach as he eyed the man. Thumhart was quite tall, at least six four. He walked like he owned the world. He sported a buzz cut, and a distinct permanent sneer.

"I'm guessing this would be him," Tom said. Greg didn't respond.

"Ah, Detective Mullins, we meet again. What a pleasure," Thumhart said, with an obvious snigger.

"Detective Alex Thumhart, this is Officer Tom O'Hara," Greg said, in way of introductions.

"Nice to meet you." Tom stood and offered his hand.

"Ummm, yeah," was Thumhart's response.

"Or not," said Tom, withdrawing his hand.

"Gentlemen, I should not be here long. I reviewed the case, and I'm working on a warrant for Winston Barnstead."

"What?" Tom and Greg blared in unison.

"Oh, gentleman, please. I know Greg went to school with the man and he's one of your own, but, goodness. Any fool could see he has to be guilty. Who else would know enough to get all the lights to go out like that?"

"Barnstead was in the room when the lights went out," Greg snarled.

"But of course he was," Thumhart snarled back in return. "He has an accomplice. That, dear gentlemen, is the rub. Once I ascertain who that is," he wiped his hands together, "it's all finished. Bing, bang, boom, done."

Greg wanted to throttle the man. Tom turned and went back to work, clearly trying to distance himself from this train wreck. "Good luck with that," Greg said, as he stood and strode out the front door.

CHAPTER 14

Rose was up early. She was a woman on a mission. "Rose," Henry said, "have you seen the glass I just put down? I think I'm losing my mind."

"What glass?"

"My coffee mug. The one Terry gave me last Christmas."

"Oh, I washed it," Rose said.

"Washed it? I just put it down to go to the bathroom. My stars, Rosey."

"I thought you were done."

"Done, how could I be done? I hadn't taken a sip out of it yet. I was letting it cool for a second. Didn't it seem a bit full to you?"

"Well, now that you mention it. I just assumed that maybe you were cutting back on caffeine like the doctor said."

"It was decaf, Rose. D-e-c-a-f, decaf. Remember making it for me about 15 minutes ago?"

"Oh, well, there's more in the pot. Help yourself. I need to get over to Fair Meadows. I have visiting to do!"

"You mean snooping. You need to go easy. You don't want Greg to be put off."

"Well, you've got a lot of nerve, Henry Sanders. You helped out with the last mystery, and now you want me to butt out. Oh, the nerve of you," Rose barked, clenched fists on her hips.

"That mystery didn't seem to involve murder, at the time. It was about the history of the house. They are two different things."

"You are welcome to come with me, if you want to involve yourself. If not, just step aside. Bruce, regardless of what he did in high school, could be in harm's way. I like the boy."

Henry regarded her carefully. He sighed. "Just hold on and I'll get dressed. I'm going to pour myself another cup of decaf, and don't you dare lay a finger on my cup!"

Rose rolled her eyes and sat down. "Fine, but be quick about it."

Henry went upstairs. Rose smiled. *That worked out better than I expected,* she thought. *I was wondering how I was going to get him to come with me without dawdling. I guess I've still got it!*

Walking into Fair Meadows, they were greeted by wonderful Christmas lights, music, a decorated tree, and a nativity set. "Wow, it looks so wonderfully festive," Rose said. "I miss having Tea here. It was always fun to walk in and wonder what he was going to say."

"Now all you have to do is walk next door," Henry said. "What's to miss?"

"Oh, I don't know. I just miss having him here, I guess. He is a dickens, isn't he?"

"Well, that's certainly one word for it," Henry mused.

"Here we are! Yooohoooo."

Rose looked toward the sound of the voice and there was Katie Wiggins, Maude Despard, Hattie Mullins, and a man Rose couldn't quite place.

"Well, hello, all. I was just remarking how truly festive it is here."

"Oh, yes," said Hattie. "I swear that once we were all asleep on Thanksgiving night, the Christmas elves all showed up. We woke up to this!" she said, her arm sweeping the room.

"Rose, Henry, I'm not sure if you remember Walter Nissan. He used to be the principal of the high school," Maude Despard said.

Henry snapped his fingers. "By gum! I knew you looked familiar. Of course I remember. We cheered the football team on, weekend after weekend."

"That we did. Sadly, it isn't quite as good now. Still, I miss the days of sitting out in the brisk Maine fall weather, yelling, 'Run, run, run!'"

"Oh, yes," said Henry. "I believe we threw a few expletives in there as well!"

"Of course! Had to light a fire under 'em. Gosh, those were the days. Bunch of wussies now, I'm afraid. Have to hide behind their mommies' skirts. It's too hot. It's too cold. My back hurts. My nose is runny. Bah! No wonder they're suckin' pond water!"

"Well, times are certainly different now. People are more safety conscious as well," Henry said.

"Yes, and I'm all for safety. I just think kids have no real guts and gumption these days. They want it all handed to them. My father rode a bike 16 miles one way to work when he was young. Kids won't do that now. If it's not easy, it's not done. It's downright scary, if you ask me."

"It was a different time then. The American spirit was different. We can't go back, so there's no use complaining," Maude explained.

"True, true. Henry, there's a nice exhibit around the corner of memorabilia from the high school. Wanna take a look?" Walter asked.

"I would love it! Lead the way."

"Maudy, would you like to come along?" Walter asked.

"Sure. I need the exercise. A little nostalgia is always pleasant."

Once the three were around the corner, Hattie said to Rose, "That's Maude's beau. He thinks she's the bee's knees. He was so kind to her when all that hoopla about Carl started a few months back. He comes across as a curmudgeon, but he's a softie at heart."

"I'm glad," Rose said. "Speaking of Carl, what's going on with that? I don't like to ask Maude. There's been nothing in the paper."

"Maude told me just yesterday that since so much time has passed, and given the circumstances, it looks like he and Sam Brinker will get parole. It's all very hush-hush. Sam Brinker is like a new man. Once that was off his chest, it was like he was literally born again. It's nice to see," Katie Wiggins said. "On another subject, I'm sure you know the police don't seem to think my son, Sam, had anything to do with that murder at the reunion. Dreadful business! Rose, what's wrong?"

Rose sank down into one of the overstuffed chairs. "Oh, there's so much more to this story, Katie. Some of it even your son doesn't know. I'll wait until Maude gets back to fill you in. I just realized how tired I am. I'm fine, really, just tired."

"Well," Katie continued, "Sam did tell me that there was another murder and there's nothing on the news about it. I found that very odd."

Before Rose could answer, Henry, Maude and Walter returned. "Come along, sit, sit, sit," Hattie said, shooing them into chairs. "Rosey was just about to fill us in on the latest happenings. She was waiting for you."

Maude and Walter obediently plunked down. Henry stood behind Rose's chair, his hand resting on its back.

Rose went through the whole story, from Bruce coming to stay with them to the Molotov cocktail being thrown through the window.

"Mercy me!" Hattie said when Rose was finished. "How absolutely terrible for you."

"Henry, I'm thankful you were okay," Maude added.

Rose looked at Katie. Rose chose not to mention Donna's rape because she wasn't sure Katie knew. Katie had her head down. She looked up and looked Rose in the eye.

"There's more to this story, and frankly, I'm done hiding it. What Rose didn't tell you was that Donna was raped by Bobby, Bruce, and Chris. It was May of their senior year. Her parents didn't know until the other night when Bruce told them. Sam called me to tell me because he wanted me to hear it from him. However, I already knew because Donna had told me. She told me and Sylvia Nitmeyer. We kept our mouths shut because Donna wanted it that way. Sam and Sarah don't even know I knew, so please don't say anything. Now, I'm going to tell you something else. Please don't repeat it for 24 hours. I want to give my family time to come forward."

Everyone nodded. Rose could barely breathe. *What on earth?* she wondered.

"Donna had a baby. The baby was adopted by Rachelle and Russ. It is their oldest son, Matthew. No one knew Donna had a child. After she died, a friend of hers contacted Sarah and Sam and told them she had Donna's son. Apparently, this woman was babysitting for the child the night Donna died. The woman said she didn't come forward right after the car accident because Donna never wanted the father to know about the child.

This woman was afraid the media would get wind of it and the father would come snooping around."

"Do you know who the father is?" Rose heard Henry ask from behind her chair.

"Well, I never met any of the three boys but Sam said Matthew is a dead-ringer for Bruce."

"Good God!" Henry said. Oh, what a tangled web we weave."

"Yes, and my son was afraid to tell anyone because he was afraid it would give the police an idea he might have a motive, and Matty doesn't know about the rape. He only knows his mom was killed and Rachelle and Russ adopted him. Until the other night, no one but me knew about the rape. Of course, Rachelle had to admit that she knew who the father had to be. Rachelle and Russ left to go back home. It was too likely that something would come out."

"So, there could be other rape victims," Walter said.

"Bruce swears, and I believe him, that he and Bobby were only involved in the one. Of course, Bobby could have lied, but, as I said, I believe Bruce. Bruce believed Bobby," Henry said.

"Well, you can bet your boots, without betraying your confidence, Katie, I'm gonna look into what Coach has been up to. I'm sure Sam Brinker can find something out. He's been tutoring math at the high school. It's possible there are more girls out there and more children. This is just horrifying for me. I swear, I never got wind of it," Walter said.

"Walter," Maude said calmly. "Be careful not to over-commit. Walter is playing Santa this year. He's volunteering at the children's hospital. He's also a substitute Santa at the mall," Maude explained.

"It's the only time this belly's come in handy," Walter chuckled.

"I think that's wonderful," Rose said. "What a great thing to do. Especially the hospital. Although, I think it would be a little sad."

"Sometimes it's quite sad," Walter said. "I've done it for a few years now. Some of the children who sat on my lap died before Christmas. It breaks my heart. It does make me happy to know I brought some happiness to them before they passed," he added.

Rose took out a tissue and wiped her eyes. "Sorry," she whispered. "If I had a dying child, I would want Santa to do just that. Santa should bring whatever happiness he can at Christmas."

CHAPTER 15

Terry was relaxing in the upstairs sitting room. Tea's cage sat beside her on the table. "Tea, I'm so glad it's Monday. I don't know about you, buddy, but these last three days have seemed like a year."

"Where's the hottie?" Tea squawked.

Terry laughed and looked at her watch. "My guess is that my hottie is at work. Tea, I think it embarrasses him when you call him a hottie. Do you think you could stop that?"

Tea blinked at her, seemingly unphased; then he turned and looked out the window.

Karen stuck her head in the door. "Hey, Shannon and I are going to do some shopping. Actually, we're paying a social call on Penny Hampton. I saw some of the note cards that she does for sale in the shop across the street. I really like them. I think the photographs are amazing. I think they're perfect for just about anything. I heard people talking about them the last few days while I was serving. I want to see if she'll let us sell some of them on consignment."

"Sounds good to me. I also think we need to have Rose get some of the tea cozies the seniors make. I think they'll make some perfect Christmas gifts."

"Ya know, I hear people talking at the tables about not even owning a teapot. I can't imagine that. I think we need to think about doing some teas out in the community. Having tea isn't just about drinking a hot beverage. It's the whole experience of it. I'm realizing people don't understand that. It's a dying art, like knitting."

Terry stared at her sister. "I can't believe my living-in-the-fast-lane sister just said that. I thought you thought of this as a quaint little business. I didn't realize you were turning into a tea activist."

"It's the tea and trade magazines. They're so cool. They have all kinds of neat decorating ideas, recipes, and information about all sorts of teas." Terry noticed Karen's whole face lit up. "There's a whole tea world out there we need to explore. I'm not really an activist. I think I'm becoming a tea fanatic, so many things to learn. I'm soaking it up like a sponge."

The door opened downstairs. Karen leaned back and looked. "Hey, you," she said, "Why aren't you at work?"

Terry heard Greg's voice say, "I took a half day today. I just got done putting some decorations up for my mom." His footsteps clomped on the stairs.

"Well, I'm on my way out with Shannon. TTFN."

There was a fluttering from Tea's cage. "Two turtle doves, three French hens," he squawked.

"Merry Christmas to you, too," Greg said. He leaned over and gave Terry a kiss.

"Cool it," Tea shrieked .

Greg sat down on the couch. "Why so glum, chum?" Terry asked, cuddling up to him.

"Greenley assigned a major league jerk to help," he said, making air quotations with his fingers around the word *help*. "His name is Alex Thumhart. I've come across him before. The fool thinks Winston Barnstead is one of the killers."

"But Winston was in the room when the lights went out."

"True, but it did dawn on me that the lights going out may not be related to Chris's murder."

Terry thought for a moment. "This is true. Did you find anyone who saw Chris after the lights went out?"

"I didn't do that part of the investigation, but Burdick said that no one remembered seeing him. It doesn't mean he wasn't around. Who knows?"

"Well, if it isn't related, it's a bizarre coincidence, given the fact that Sandy was whacked over the head with a bottle."

"Tom told me that Thumhart's theory is that whoever killed Chris got him out of there by gun point while the lights were out. An accomplice was waiting. They drugged him and shot him."

"Drugged him?" Terry asked.

"Oh, crap. I forgot you didn't know. Don't repeat this, but there was rohypnol in his system. The guy was probably out cold. It makes sense because Sandy remembers him suddenly letting go of her hand and starting to lean a little forward. That's when the lights went out."

"So, it was probably in his drink, right?" Terry asked. "Then Thumhart's theory makes no sense because if Chris's drink was drugged and Chris passed out, he didn't walk out of there at gun point. He would have to have been carried. Don't ya think we might have noticed Chris's body going by us? Duh!"

Greg's phone rang and he looked at the caller ID. "Tom," he told her, answering the phone. "Yeah," Greg said, taking a deep breath.

Terry watched his face. He frowned and then his eyes grew wide.

"Is he insane? How in the world did he come up with that?" Greg's voice was tense. He was quiet for a bit. "It was definitely Chris's hair?" he asked, and listened some more.

"Well, now we know how he got out of there. Okay. Let me know what else Dumbo does. Also, let me know if he gets the arrest warrant." Shaking his head, he ended the call and turned to Terry. "This just gets worse. Thumhart's *new* theory is that Sandy drugged the drink. The bartender said she thought she saw a woman coming up by Sandy. Thumhart believes it was Winston's wife. He thinks she handed the drug off to Sandy. He believes the Barnsteads and Sandy are a team."

"Are you kidding me? She was so sweet. Besides, if they were a team, why would they hurt Sandy?"

"Thumhart's theory is that they hit Sandy over the head to draw suspicion away from her involvement. Once the lights went out, Barnstead snuck up and pulled Chris's body aside. They waited until people were out of the room, and then put Chris in the dumbwaiter."

"Dumbwaiter? When did a dumbwaiter come into the picture?"

"They found some of Chris's hair in the dumbwaiter. Someone did use the dumbwaiter to get him down to the garage level. According to Thumhart, while Sandy was being loaded into the ambulance, one Barnstead activated the dumbwaiter while the other waited to load him in the car. It isn't a bad theory as far as things go, but there's no way the Barnsteads could have pulled it off. Besides, Sandy is hysterical. No way she was in on it," Greg said, shaking his head. "It's just like he's done before. Thumhart gets some things right, and then zips off in the wrong direction. True, someone must have drugged Chris and put him in the dumbwaiter. True, he must have gone from the dumbwaiter to a car. After that, the theory makes no sense."

"So, I guess we need to clear Winston," Terry said.

"What? No! That's not what I'm saying. There isn't even a warrant yet. It just ticks me off that Thumhart is wasting time like this while the real killer, or killers, have a chance to be long gone."

"Did they find the gun?" Terry asked.

"Nope."

"Well, I think you and Bruce should go have a chat with Coach. If anyone knows who else was raped, it would be him. Right?"

Greg looked at her. "Yeah, I suppose that's a good idea."

"Idiot," said Tea. "Three French hens."

"Tea wants this case settled by Christmas," Terry said.

"I'm already calling Bruce and Tom," Greg said, cell phone in hand.

"Electric slide," Tea squawked.

Greg looked questioningly at Terry. She shrugged. "Perhaps he's just a party animal," she suggested.

CHAPTER 16

Greg was standing next to his car in front of Coach's house when Tom pulled up in a cruiser.

"Thumhart thinks something's up," Tom said, getting out of the police car.

"And your neighborhood probably thinks I'm under arrest," Bruce said, getting out of the passenger side.

Greg imagined his neighbors peeking out of their windows, watching as Tom went to pick up Bruce. "Yeah, my neighbors are all probably on their phones now," Greg said. "Tom, what did you tell Thumhart?"

"I told him nothing. He's technically nothing to me. I just said I'd be back in a few."

"So why do you think he's suspicious?" Greg asked.

"He was hovering when you called me. As I was leaving, he said, 'I can be your best friend or your worst nightmare.' A bit dramatic, don't ya think?"

"Don't turn your back on him," Greg warned. "He's a snake. He's caused a lot of trouble for some State Police guys. None of us know how he charms the higher-ups."

Bruce nodded toward the house. "Coach just looked out that front window. He knows we're out here. We might as well get this over with."

As the three men trudged toward the brick house with green shutters and snow-covered bushes, the front door swung open. "Well, well, well, I see Wilson is still alive."

"Yup, and I want to keep it that way," Bruce answered. "We want to ask you some questions about stuff in high school."

"Why bring the *po-leeeese?*" Coach asked.

Greg took notice of the man's disheveled appearance, and the slight slurring of his speech. His graying hair was unwashed and uncombed. His shirt wasn't buttoned correctly, and his pants were stained and had multiple cigarette burns. "Actually, we brought Bruce. We think that the two of you can help us figure this out. Between his memory and yours, there has to be a lead there somewhere," Greg answered.

"I already know who it is," Coach said. "She don't look like much, but she sure has some balls on her."

Greg and Bruce exchanged glances. From behind them, Tom asked, "Well, then can we come in and have you fill us in on what you know?"

Coach was silent for a beat. Greg wasn't sure he was going to let them in, but Coach stepped aside and gestured for them to enter.

What a mess! Greg thought, looking around. There were wall-to-wall food delivery boxes and beer bottles. A half empty bottle of vodka sat on a table in front of the couch right next to a glass filled with an orange liquid. Greg looked around for a place to sit, but dirty clothes and newspapers covered the chairs.

"Just toss the stuff on the floor and make yourselves at home. My maid has the day off." Coach chuckled at his own joke.

Tom and Greg sat on two navy blue wing-backed chairs. Bruce sat down on the couch, next to Coach. "Okay, Coach. Who's behind this? Who wants us dead?" Bruce asked.

"It's that stupid wench we screwed years ago on the beach, Brucey," Coach answered. "You must remember her. She was your first, as I recall." Coach guffawed and slapped Bruce's leg. "You haven't forgotten, have you?"

Bruce hung his head and slowly shook it. "She's dead, Coach. She died years ago."

"Yeah, well, before she supposedly died, she came to visit me. She brought that friend of hers. What was his name? Oh, yeah, Weaver. Two of them wanted money from me. She said she was pregnant with twins."

"Twins?" Bruce and Greg asked in unison.

"Yeah, twins. She said she got pregnant that night. Like I would believe her! I told her that Weaver was probably the father and, until I had a blood test, I wasn't giving her a flippin' dime."

"Did she come back with the blood tests?" Bruce asked, a sense of urgency in his voice. "Did she really have twins?"

"Never heard from the little whore again. She was all emotional, crying her little baby blues out. She said she couldn't even bear to face her family."

"What would make you think it was her?" Tom asked. "After all these years, and the fact that she died in a car accident."

"No one else it could be," Coach said. "Plenty o' people hate me, but those boys never gave anyone reason. You all were kinda wussies. If it isn't her or Weaver, it's got to be her family."

Bruce stood up, his face flaming in anger. "Wussies? Chris looked up to you. Thought of you as a second father, and you call him a wussie! You called Bobby a few times a month. He thought you really cared about him. What is wrong with you, man?" Bruce looked at Greg. "Do you think we ever knew this guy?" he asked.

"I kept tabs on all you guys, 'specially you and Bobby. You and he went all soft on me. Giving money every year to the fund in that little tramp's name. I was worried you were gonna rat on us. Bein' that these two police fellas didn't blink a few minutes ago, or even ask a question, tells me they know about out little play date on the beach."

"You're damn right they know," Bruce screamed. "They know because I apologized to the Wiggins family for what we did. I also told the police, in case you did it to someone else. How many were raped, Coach? How many humiliated girls did you leave in your wake? You didn't tell us she was pregnant. All these years, you've said nothing. You raped her as well. It's not like you were just the cheerleader. What if the babies were one of ours? Maybe we aren't as sleazy as you. Bobby and I would have wanted to know!"

Greg stood and put a hand on Bruce's shoulder. Bruce's face showed pure fury. Greg supposed, at that moment, Bruce could kill Coach with his bare hands. "Easy, we'll sort it out. We'll talk to the Weavers. Calm down."

"How many others were there, Coach?" Tom asked. "How many other girls and their families could want you dead?"

"None that concern any of you," Coach sneered. "Do you really think Bobby and this pansy could stomach another play date?" he asked Tom, pointing to Bruce.

"What about Chris?" Bruce asked, with a note of disgust.

"Naw, he was too enamored with you and Cooper. I think he had a man crush on you two. Always talking about you guys. When Bobby's wife had those kids, the man went gaga. Said he needed to change. Jerk."

For a brief moment, Greg felt sorrow well up in his gut. Chris wasn't what he appeared. He wanted to be a better person. He envied Bobby and Bruce. Maybe, if someone hadn't killed him? He quickly shoved those feelings away, to be dealt with another time. His cell rang. He looked at the caller ID. It was a local number. It seemed familiar, but he couldn't place it. He sent the call to voicemail. It could wait.

"Well, Coach, I guess we'll be in touch," Tom said. "Thanks for the chat. I hope your maid comes back tomorrow."

Greg was shocked Tom said that. He usually wasn't one to be sarcastic. Apparently, Coach got under his skin, too.

When they got outside to the police car, Greg stopped and took out his phone. "Before you take off, let me check my phone. I want to make sure this call isn't related." He pulled out his phone, pressed a button and listened. It was Sam Wiggins. Greg held up a finger as he listened to the message. When it was done, he said, "I'm riding with Tom. Bruce, you can take my car. Tom and I need to make another stop."

"Okay," Bruce said. "But later, we need to talk about how I can find out if Donna was pregnant. I want to know what happened to those babies."

As Bruce drove away, Greg turned to Tom. "Sam Wiggins says he needs to talk to us. He says Donna had a child. A child, not twins. He says he wants to tell us the rest of the story. This is just unbelievable."

"This whole thing is one big hornet's nest," Tom said, putting the cruiser in gear.

By the time they pulled into the Wiggins' driveway, Greg's mind was in full whirl. He couldn't believe what Wiggins had said. How could that be?"

"Okay," Tom said, "here we are."

A red-eyed Sarah Wiggins was at the door. Her normally immaculate appearance was replaced with a wilder look. She was visibly shaking. The handle of the screen door rattled in her hand. Sam appeared behind her. "Come in," he said. There was a chill to his voice.

Greg and Tom sat with the Wiggins in a very elegant room. They referred to it as a den, but it put any living room Greg had ever been in to shame. "Mr. Wiggins, your call left me a bit confused. I'd appreciate it if you'd please run through things from the top," Greg said. He was surprised at the stoniness of his own voice.

Sam Wiggins cleared his throat. "It's very simple, really. After Donna died, a woman called us and said she had Donna's child. She explained that she had kept quiet to avoid media coverage. She came here and brought Matthew."

"Matthew is the child's name?" Tom queried. The Wiggins nodded.

"The woman simply said that Donna got pregnant and was embarrassed to tell us. She didn't tell us it was rape. If she had, we would have gone to the police. We figured Donna got pregnant in high school or immediately after. We approached the Weavers. We thought Adam might be the father. Of course, Adam was dead by then, but it would have explained things. Mr. and Mrs. Weaver didn't know anything at all. Adam's sister told us that Adam had been giving Donna money each month because he wanted to help her. His sister said that Adam swore the child was not his, but wouldn't say who the father was."

"You simply cannot let this come out," Sarah said. "Matthew thinks Russ is his father. Rachelle took the child right away. She was here when the woman came. She was still in college, but we paid for daycare, and any extra help she needed. Russ was just in the picture, at that point. Matthew was three when they got married. We just lied and took a year off his age to ensure people thought the child was Russ's." Sarah's right hand continually fidgeted with her wedding ring. "We never showed anyone pictures. When their second child, Emily, was born we just continued to seem like grandparents who didn't show pictures around. It would seem strange to show pictures of one grandchild and not the other. We went to visit them often. They hardly ever came here."

"So," Greg said. "You still don't know who the father of Donna's child is?"

Sam Wiggins reached into his pocket and took out his wallet. "I don't show the picture, but I still keep one in my wallet," he explained as he handed it to Greg. Greg looked down, and drew a breath. Tom looked over and gave a whistle. They were staring at what could have been Bruce's high school picture.

"I guess you do know," Greg said. He gathered his thoughts and continued. "This may be very hard for you to hear, but Coach Walker said that Donna came to see him. She said she was pregnant with twins. Did this woman mention another child?"

Sarah gasped. Greg was sure she knew nothing about another child. The look on Sam's face told him the same. "No," Sam said. "No, no, nothing at all. Did Coach Walker see the babies? Did she contact him again?"

"No, actually, Adam Weaver was with her. Coach assumed the babies were his. Of course, I suppose Donna could have been bluffing. Maybe she was so desperate for money that she said she was having twins," Greg suggested.

"That doesn't sound like Donna at all," Sam said. Sarah was a weeping mess and simply couldn't speak. Sam continued. "Of course, I never would have thought that Donna would have kept a pregnancy from us. We were, are, such a close family. I...I don't know."

"What's the name of Donna's friend?" Tom asked. "Where was she from?"

The Wiggins looked at each other. "We honestly can't remember," Sam said. "Her first name was

Denise. That we remember. Donna was killed in Calais. We assumed she lived near there. She just dropped off Matthew. She said she was sorry we lost Donna, and that Donna was a great and caring friend. She kissed Matthew and left. Matthew was sixteen months old at the time. He saw Rachelle and said, 'Mama.' That made our decision easy."

"So, you have no idea who this woman was? At the time, how could you have been sure the child was Donna's?" Tom asked.

"Rachelle has his birth certificate. Denise gave it to us," Sam explained.

"Well," Greg said, "this may or may not relate to the murders. However, I will tell you that you need to tell Bruce. It's only fair. I can't tell him. I technically can't make you tell him. However, if it comes out as some part of this investigation, it would be better coming from you."

"Can you see if there was another baby?" Sarah managed to ask.

"No, but you can. You can contact the hospital. You could hire a private investigator. You have options."

Sarah reached out and grabbed her husband's arm. "We need to know," she whispered. He patted her hand, but said nothing.

Tom and Greg stood up, and Sam showed them out. When they were seated in the cruiser, Tom said, "If I were Bruce, I don't know what I'd do. How about you?"

"I can't even get my head around this," Greg responded. "I can see them not saying anything initially because they didn't know any of the facts. But they had the chance this weekend. Bruce told us the whole story about confessing to the Wiggins. Maybe, if I were in their shoes, I wouldn't have said anything. It's just too convoluted."

"Do you think they put it together and are somehow connected to the murder?" Tom asked.

"No, unless they're amazing actors. But, I wouldn't put it past Coach. It crossed my mind that it could be his attempt to keep things quiet. Bruce said they were going to apologize this weekend. Maybe Bobby told Coach. Maybe Chris told Coach. However, he seemed generally freaked by the deaths."

"Well, we can check his phone records to see if he received the calls he said he did. The murders may not be related to the rape," Tom said. "Although, my gut is saying they are."

"I've learned to trust your gut," Greg said. "It's served us well. All we have to do now is figure out the relationship."

"I think we need to talk to Adam Weaver's sister. She might know. Do you know her name?"

"Yeah, it's Mandy. I think she still lives in town. I'll check into it tomorrow."

"Sounds good. What are we gonna do about Thumhart?" Tom asked.

"Nothing. Absolutely nothing. If he makes an arrest, I may change my mind. But for now, let him chase his wild goose. It'll keep him busy," Greg said.

"And outta our hair," Tom added. The two men did a high-five.

CHAPTER 17

"I thought Monday, our day off, would make me feel better," Terry said to Karen. "But after last night, I just couldn't sleep." She took some blueberry scones out of the oven.

"Me neither," Karen said, getting place settings ready. "My head is still spinning. I don't blame Bruce for being angry, though. At the same time, I can understand why Rachelle didn't say anything. You don't just simply say, 'Hey, I think we have your kid.' I'm glad Bruce's father called Henry. After Bruce called him, his dad figured Bruce needed a local someone. Ter, do you think Greg feels in the middle?"

"I asked him that last night. He said that it's awkward for him because he needs to stay neutral. The whole thing suddenly blew up. Once all the secrets were out, it was like an avalanche enveloping everyone involved. Katie Wiggins told Rose and Henry about Donna having a baby. Because they knew, she told Sam Wiggins he needed to come clean to the police. Once the Wiggins told the police, the Wiggins knew they needed to tell Bruce. Russ called Bruce to tell him about Matthew. It was like a soap opera. As of right now, everyone knows Donna got pregnant, but no one knows how many babies she had. Of course, Matthew, Donna's son that Rachelle has, still has no idea that Bruce is his real father. Now, everyone's in a tizzy because they don't know if there was one child or two, if there are two, and if so, where's the other baby, and if any of this is connected to the murders. It's a very tangled web that is quickly unraveling. Greg and I talked until almost two in the morning. We both agree that the only way it can all be connected to the murders is if Donna confided in someone and that person is out for revenge on Donna's behalf. Of course, Adam Weaver could have told someone too. Either way, someone else is avenging Donna's rape. Greg is hoping Tom can check Coach's phone records today. They did put some paperwork in the other day to check Bobby's phone records. Shantel gave them the number." Terry twisted her hair back into a pony tail. "The phone was under Shantel's name anyway. The records should let them know if Coach and Bobby received the phone calls and texts they said they did. If they didn't, then that changes things."

"Man, the whole story makes my head spin. What was it you started to tell me last night about some other detective who Greg can't stand?" Karen asked, as she began taking cups out of the dishwasher.

"It's a guy named Thumhart," Terry said, taking glasses from Karen and putting them away. "He's sure Winston Barnstead is the murderer. He believes that Winston is the only one who had enough information to engineer all the lights going out in the hotel. He thinks Sandy might be in on it, too. He thinks Sandy and Winston are in cahoots. Greg just wants Thumhart to stay out of his way."

The kitchen door opened, and Shannon walked in. "Sorry I'm a few minutes late. My mom got a call from your Aunt Rose. Then, she needed to fill me in. Sheesh, a day for the rest of us is like a month in your world. Is Greg going to help Bruce figure out if there were twins?"

"Right now, he needs to figure out who's killing people. The babies are a whole other issue. Greg says the Wiggins can hire a private investigator."

"Doesn't he care?" Shannon asked.

"It's not about caring; it's about what cases he's been assigned. He can't just decide to try and figure out what happened all those years ago. That's really up to the Wiggins and Bruce. Rachelle is going to let Bruce meet Matthew. Of course, she first has to explain to Matthew that he believed a lie all these years. I don't know the details about when this meeting will take place. I just know it's gonna happen."

"I haven't had time to talk to Tom this morning. I talked to him last night, but he didn't say anything. He couldn't. I don't think he knew that the lid blew off things. He did mention some annoyance called Thumhart."

"And that's another story," Karen added.

"It's a story that's gonna have to wait," Terry said. "We've got two bridge clubs coming today. We've got work to do. After we close, I'll fill you in."

"It's a deal," Shannon said.

It turned out the bridge clubbers were a lively group. There was so much laughter and chatting that Terry felt refreshed. The air vibrated with happiness. It was fun to see the teahouse with its Christmas lights twinkling. The poinsettia and candy cane centerpieces were a hit. "I just love these holiday menus you have," one woman said. "It's so fun to see the little characters you painted on the walls now decorating your menu, but all dressed-up for Christmas. I love this little mouse in the Santa outfit."

"My favorite is the goose with elf shoes and the elf hat on," said another.

Mr. Tea, as always, was a hit. He sang 'Jingle Bells,' and rang his bell. "Santa's coming, watch yourselves," he squawked. The biggest hit was "Pucker up, Santa Baby." Karen played Christmas CDs as quiet background music. When "Jingle Bell Rock" played, Tea hammed it up. People even got up from their seats to go stand in the waiting doorway and watch. It was a fantastic start to their Christmas season.

"I can't wait to spread the word," a woman, wearing a holiday sweater with blinking colored lights, said. "Everyone should have their Christmas gatherings right here."

"Thank you," Terry said. "It's nice to know you enjoyed yourself."

"Nice lights, toots," Tea said.

The woman and her friends laughed their way out the front door.

About two o'clock, things quieted down. The three women sat in the kitchen, sampling various Christmas teas. "I think my favorite is the one called "Sugar Plum Delight." It's sweet without being too sweet," Karen said.

"I think my favorite is "Peppermint Dreams." It reminds me of candy canes," Terry said.

"I can't make up my mind," Shannon said. "I enjoyed them all."

"Terry," Karen said. "I've been thinking. Do you think there's any chance that Donna's and Adam Weaver's car accidents weren't really accidents?"

"Karen, I was enjoying myself. Don't bring that stuff up. I can't think about it now," Terry groaned.

"Do you think they could be related?" Shannon asked, looking wide-eyed at Karen. "I'm sorry, Terry. I just think that's quite an idea. Can't we talk about it until someone comes in?"

"Whatever," Terry said, flipping her hand. "If the police didn't suspect foul play in the accidents, why would you?"

"The police didn't know what we know."

"Who could possibly have caused both accidents?" asked Terry, exasperated.

"Coach," Karen said. "We only have his word that he never heard from Donna again. What if Donna and Adam Weaver were blackmailing him?"

"What if they were? How would that relate to Bobby's and Chris's deaths? Besides, I repeat, how could we prove their deaths weren't accidents?"

"Just a thought," Karen said.

At that moment, the front door jingled. "Saved by the bell," Terry said.

Bruce Wilson came in and looked around. He leaned back so he could see into the parlor/waiting room. He waved at Tea. "Hey, buddy. You're the talk of the town."

"Hi," Karen said, getting up. "What brings you to this part of town, stranger?"

"My mother wanted me to take a look at some quilts across the street. I have no idea why. I'm a guy. It goes on the bed. It's a blanket, a bedspread, whatever. I never think of them as art."

"Oh, but they can be," Terry said. "They can be amazing works of art. Slaves used them to guide others to the Underground Railroad. There's a quilting museum."

"It's kind of like that Oldsmobile commercial from years ago. 'It's not your father's Oldsmobile," Karen said, grinning.

Terry rolled her eyes. "I take it your mother is having you look at the Annabelle Rhodes quilts."

"Yeah, how did you know?"

"She lives close to here. I heard she was doing some for the shop across the street. I haven't had a chance to go see them. What is your mother looking for?"

Bruce got out his cell phone and scrolled through some things. Then he held up a picture of a living room for Terry to see. "Something with blue that would go in this room," he said, shrugging.

"Would you like me to go across with you and give you my opinion?" Terry asked.

"Sure! That would help lots. I really just don't get it," Bruce confessed.

"Me neither," Karen added. "Mind if I come along? I'd like to see what all the fuss is about. Shannon, can you hold down the fort for a few?"

"Of course. No one's here. That, I can handle," Shannon said.

As they trudged down the driveway, Bruce said to Karen, "Do you miss the warm weather you had in California?"

Karen thought a moment. "Actually, I'm surprised to say, no. I thought I would, but I don't. Maybe it's because I don't have to travel to work. It could be because Christmas is coming. Ask me in March, and my answer might change."

"Do you ski?" Bruce asked.

"I used to. I love snowmobiling. Do you? Ski, I mean."

"Yeah. I love it, downhill and cross country. I even snowmobile. Greg and I were talking about snowmobiling last night. We were thinking of getting a bunch of us together to go," Bruce said. "Would you ladies like to join us?"

"Sure," Karen said, before Terry could open her mouth. That was okay because Terry highly suspected the invitation was directed more toward Karen. She thought back to the other night when Henry's house was on fire. They were all panicking, trying to get Karen and Rose out of the bush and away from the house. A brief image of Bruce setting Karen down and looking at her to make sure she was okay floated into Terry's mind. She didn't think about it at the time, but there was something about the look on his face. *Maybe,* she mused. She wasn't sure how she felt about that. The man raped a woman. Granted, he seemed genuinely sorry, but still. Terry made a mental note to think more about it later. Did it bother Karen? It should.

Bruce held the door open for them and they walked in. It was a gift shop for people who preferred hand-crafted items. Nothing here was cheap. Still, the store emitted warmth, like cookies right out of the oven. Terry waved to the owner, Cheryl, as she followed Bruce back toward the quilts.

"Ahhh, he went for back-up," Cheryl said. "You had a dubious look about you," she said to Bruce.

"Yeah, sorry. To me, a blanket's a blanket," Bruce said.

Terry studied the quilts. She felt like the proverbial kid in a candy store. Her heart was racing with delight. The colors and textures swirled in her mind. She turned to Bruce. "Can I see the picture again?"

"Sure." He found it and held it up for her to study. She noted the blues, creams, and corals in the room. She squinted at the photo as she held it up to her face. She turned back to the quilts, noting their subtleties. She looked at Bruce and Karen. Their faces were blank. They wore the 'I got nothin' look.

"There's one here that will fit perfectly," Terry said. "Karen, think carefully. Take a look at the room and make a guess."

Karen's face turned to 'deer in the headlights.' She glanced at Bruce and slunk forward. She looked at the picture in Bruce's hand. Terry watched her waver between three. One of them was the right choice. There was hope.

"This one," she said tentatively.

"Yes," said Terry. Karen picked the quilt with a dark red background with flowers that went around the outer edges of the quilt. The background for the main design was a pastel yellow with splotches of pinks, oranges, corals, and darker yellows. The design looked like a watercolor. There were six hexagons done in light blues, the red with floral background color, and a blue flowered pattern that looked like it was taken from a Monet pattern. The center of each hexagon held a yellow or dark red square. Each side of the squares was the bottom of a parallelogram made up of blues and dark reds. Terry knew it would play up the blues and tie in the yellows and browns in the room.

Cheryl burst out laughing. "That's the one he was thinking about!"

Bruce shrugged.

"See?" Terry said. "There's hope for you two yet."

Bruce took a picture of the quilt and sent it to his mother. She called him back immediately and gushed over it. The details were worked out and payment made. On their way out of the shop, Bruce's phone rang. He looked down at it. "Gotta take this," he said. "Go ahead back, I'll stop by," he said, followed by "Hello?" into his phone.

"Nice guy," Terry said to Karen. "He's had quite the week. Wouldn't you say?"

"I can't even imagine," Karen said. "His two closest friends are murdered, and he finds out he has a son. I'm surprised he's still walking and talking. I'd be a mess."

"Well, look what you went through with Mom's death and your divorce. You and he are the type of people who somehow manage to cope. He seems to like you. How do you feel about that?"

"I'm trying not to think about it, actually. I was touched by his close relationship to his mother, but—"

"But?"

"But I keep thinking about Donna. What they did to her disgusts me. That could have been me. It just happened to be her that night. I can't imagine dealing with that. I keep wondering how they could do something like that. I think about Shantel and wonder how she got past that with Bobby. I know people change, but some people never really do. Remember when Mom died and we talked a little bit about forgiveness being God's job?"

"Yeah, I vaguely remember Pastor's sermon about it."

"Well, I need to do some soul searching and thinking. That's just where I am with it."

"Do you ever think about having another relationship? The divorce was rough on you." Terry said.

Karen shrugged. "Sometimes, I'm okay about the divorce. Other times, I'm furious over the time I wasted. I threw away years, waiting for us to be financially ready to have kids."

"Can't go back, just forward," Terry reminded her. "I think about the years I wasted living with Jeff. I knew he wasn't the one I wanted to marry. He felt the same way. It was just convenient. We each brought out each other's creative sides. Now my biological clock is ticking, and I keep wishing I hadn't wasted the time. Then, of course, I wouldn't have had the chance to get to know Greg." She shrugged. "Forward and onward, I guess."

Terry opened the door to Madeline's Teahouse. "Hold that door," called a voice from across the street, and Bruce dashed over. He was frowning.

"Problem?" Karen asked, stopping at the door.

"Yeah. That was Shantel. The babies seem to sense something is wrong. Little Bruce has always been a little colicky, and Bobby and I were the only ones who could calm him down," he said. "Bobby said, and I agree, it's because Shantel and her mother get rattled by the screaming. Bobby and I kinda take it in stride. Anyway, Shantel is exhausted and Bobby's parents are a mess. I gotta go over there and see if I can help."

"If they need more hands, I'm willing to pitch in," Karen said. "I had a friend in California with a colicky baby. She taught me how to keep calm through the screaming. I babysat when she needed a break."

"I think that would be great," Bruce said. "Let me give Shantel a call back." He took out his cell phone and walked back down the walkway. Terry knew it was for better cell phone reception. That was one problem of living in a small town.

"All's quiet," Shannon said, as they entered the teahouse.

"That's good," Karen said. "Do you think you and Terry can hold down the fort if I go with Bruce to help Shantel with the triplets? I guess it's a little hard over at Bobby's parents' house."

"We close soon anyway," Shannon said. "I'm willing to help if she needs it."

"I guess I can help, too," Terry said. "I've done my share of babysitting."

Karen opened the door and looked out. "Hold on a minute," she said as she ran over to Bruce.

Terry looked at Shannon. "Bruce said one of the babies is colicky. Are you up for that?"

Shannon shrugged. "If it gets to me, there's always Henry's margaritas. Besides, it's the least we can do. Her husband was murdered."

"True," Terry said, as Karen came back inside.

"It's a go. They need all the help they can get," Karen said.

***

Bruce pulled up to the curb in front of the blue and brick colonial with black shutters. Terry saw Shantel standing at the bay window, patting the back of a red-faced baby. Terry realized she could hear babies crying all the way at the end of the driveway.

"Ah, the sweet music of life," Bruce said. His face became downcast. "That's what Bobby used to say."

"Wow," Shannon said. "That's a good way to look at it."

"Yeah, Bobby said he never thought he'd get a chance at a life with someone like Shantel after what we did in high school. He was afraid to hope for anything more. The triplets were a bonus—a gift." He stopped and cleared his throat. He took a deep breath as he looked up at the sky. "This is hard," he whispered. I gotta get it together for their sake." He gestured toward the house.

The front door opened and Mrs. Wilson, Bobby's mom, stood there with another crying baby. *The poor woman,* Terry thought, noticing the dark circles under her eyes, the harried look on her face, and her uncombed hair.

A dog scooted out from behind her and took off down the driveway toward them. "Bertha, inside," Bruce said, pointing to the house.

"Bertha?" Karen queried.

"Oh, heck yeah," Bruce answered, as they walked toward the house. "Her original name was Princess. Shantel named her. They only had her a week when Chris and I came to visit. It was a three-hour drive for Chris and he picked me up on the way. Anyway, Chris and I were sittin' out on the front porch on Saturday morning, drinking coffee. Bobby opened the door to come out and join us and the dog darted out and took off down the sidewalk. That dang dog was wearin' a little pink tutu Shantel had put on her. Bobby went up and down that sidewalk, calling, 'Here, Princess. Here, Princess. Come here. Come here, Princess.' Chris and I just about wet ourselves, laughing so hard. Shantel came out, took one look, and shot coffee out her nose. Well, needless to say, Bobby was mad as mad gets. When he caught the dog and handed her back to Shantel, he said, 'There's no way I'm calling for Princess around town. The dog's name is now Bertha. If she escapes wearin' that blasted skirt, you can go get 'er!' That's how Bertha got her name. Although, we pretty much always refer to her as Bertie."

Terry chuckled. She never thought about how men must feel, chasing after dogs or cats with names like Muffin or Princess.

Mr. Wilson appeared as they entered the house. He, too, was holding a baby. The baby's lip was quivering. Another unhappy camper. Terry wondered which baby was which. "Thank God, you've all come," Mr. Wilson said. "These poor little ones have got us plum worn out."

The baby in Mrs. Wilson's arms let out a high-pitched screech. Bruce held out his arms. "Come see me, partner. It's your Uncle Bruce." Mrs. Wilson was so glad to hand over the baby that she just about tossed him at Bruce. The baby was bald as Annie's Daddy Warbucks. Terry assumed it was a boy because of the blue and white onesie with little trucks on it.

"Please come in and have a seat," Mr. Wilson said to the girls. "You've got to excuse us. This is just a terrible time. Just terrible."

"I'm sure it is," Terry said. "We're so sorry for your loss. We all liked Bobby."

Bobby's mother sniffled and left the room, obviously distraught. Terry wasn't sure what to say or do. Her heart ached for these people. She knew there were no words that would help.

"Please, sit," Shantel said, nodding toward the couch.

"Can I hold the baby for a bit?" Karen asked.

"Be my guest," Shantel said. "This is Christine. She's exhausted. Every time her brother Bruce starts crying, she feels obligated to join in."

Karen took Christine. "Well, hello, sweet girl. Look at your beautiful brown eyes." The baby studied Karen. Terry saw the little eyebrows furrow. "Are you not sure about me? Are you wondering who this funny-looking lady is? I don't blame you. I wonder that every time I look in the mirror. I love your Minnie Mouse dress. It's so pretty." The baby smiled and Shantel laughed.

"That's a very good sign," Shantel said. "She can be a little hard to win over."

Terry turned and saw Mr. Wilson behind her. "May I?" she asked, tentatively holding out her arms.

"Be my guest," Mr. Wilson said. Terry took the uncertain baby. "That's Robby," Mr. Wilson said, his eyes tearing up. Robby looked over at his brother Bruce who was still wailing in Bruce's arms. Robby turned back to Terry. She smiled at him. He had beautiful big brown eyes and lovely long lashes. He was wearing a blue and white onesie with airplanes. "Oh, you are a cutie-pie. You're going to be a heart-throb with those eyes," Terry said. She gently kissed his little forehead. She saw his little lip start to quiver. Terry puffed out her cheeks and made a face at him. He stared at her. She scrunched up her nose and made another face. The corner of his mouth twitched. He was clearly unsure whether or not to smile. Terry sat on the couch next to Karen. Robby looked at his sister. She smiled back at him. He looked at Terry, then back at Christine who clapped her hands and smiled again.

"See," Terry said. "She thinks we have potential." Robby smiled.

"While they are somewhat content, I am going to go make bottles," Shantel said.

"I'll help," Shannon said. "I can be an extra pair of hands."

"I'm going to go check on my wife," Mr. Wilson said. "The two of us don't mean to be rude, but we really need a nap."

"That's why we're here," Bruce said.

"And we really appreciate it, let me tell you," Mr. Wilson replied. He went off down the hall.

Terry realized it was suddenly quiet. She looked over toward Bruce. The baby was sniveling, but seemed momentarily content. Bruce sat down in a rocking recliner and started to rock. "See, little friend. It's okay."

This is incredibly peaceful, Terry thought. Bertha sat in front of Terry and Karen. She cocked her head to the side. She looked over at Bruce.

"It's okay, Bertie, girl. They're with me. They won't hurt your babies," Bruce told the dog. Bertha flopped down as if to say, *Phew, a moment of peace and quiet in this place!*

"How old are they?" Karen asked.

"Eight months," Bruce answered.

Shantel and Shannon returned and handed out bottles. The triplets gladly took them. Shantel sat down with a deep sigh. "Again, I can't thank you enough," she said, looking at Bruce. "My poor in-laws. When Bobby's mother found out, she became hysterical, understandably, and it woke the babies. They've pretty much screamed for most of the time since then. They scream until they're exhausted, and then they conk out for about two to three hours and then it starts up again. It's been Hell. I didn't know what else to do but call you."

"You can always call me, Shannie," Bruce said.

"Well, I know that, but you have your own problems. You loved him, too. The funeral will be next weekend. Bobby's sister was so upset that she started having contractions. She isn't due for another two months. His parents want to give her time to calm down. His aunts and uncles will be flying in later this week. Money is a problem for some of them and Bobby's dad is wiring money or buying tickets. I'm not sure which. Speaking of problems, what happened to Chris?"

Terry, Karen, and Shannon all exchanged glances. Terry saw Bruce looking down at the floor.

"What? What's wrong?" Shantel asked, obviously picking up on their body language. "You said Chris couldn't answer his phone because he had some issues. Bruce, what happened?"

"Shannie, Chris was murdered last night," Bruce said, his voice shaky.

"What?" Shantel jumped up. Then Bertha jumped up and barked. The triplets looked around, wide-eyed. Shantel, quickly sat down again. "It's okay, Bertie. It's okay." There were a few moments of silence. The triplets seemed to be watching the dog. When Bertie flopped back down, the triplets went back to sucking on their bottles. "Oh, my sweet Jesus," Shantel whispered. "How? When? I can't even think straight about this."

"He was killed after the reunion dinner. We're still getting the details. The police are keeping it quiet until his family is notified."

Shantel stared off into space for a moment. "It has to be connected to Bobby's murder. It has to be—" She stopped. She clearly didn't want to continue.

"It's okay; I told them. I had to. It's too long of a story to go into right now."

Terry noticed that Shantel looked relieved. Standing up, she said, "Does anyone mind if I play the piano? I feel the need to play the song for Bobby's funeral."

"You're gonna try and sing at Bobby's funeral?" Bruce asked, incredulously. "How can you possibly get through it?"

Before Shantel could answer, Shannon asked, "What song is it?"

"It's a song written by a friend of mine. It became Bobby's favorite song. When we first started dating, he wasn't a believer. He thought there was no hope for forgiveness. He just hated himself." She stopped and shook her head. "He knew I was a believer, so he acquiesced to going to church with me. One Sunday, after church, we were in my car and, without thinking, I put the CD in. This song came on and Bobby broke down in tears. He suddenly understood the immensity of God's grace."

"It changed his life," Bruce said. "Actually, all of our lives. He made Chris and me listen to it the next time we saw him. I'm not kidding when I say that we made him play it over and over. We listened to that song at least ten times that one day. Chris paced up and down the porch. He kept waving his hand and sayin' 'It's too good to be true.' You wouldn't know it to see how he acted, but Chris was thrown by that song. For the first time, I saw him have real shame about the way he treated women. As big a jerk as he could be, he was getting better." Bruce's voice caught.

Shantel stood up and took the sleeping baby from his arms. She put little Bruce in the baby swing. "Play," she said, nodding at the piano.

"I don't know if I can get through it, Shannie. Bobby's death is recent, my grief too new."

"Try."

Bruce got up and went to the piano. Shantel sat next to him. Terry shot a sidelong glance at Karen. This was such a personal moment between Bruce and Shantel. Terry felt like an intruder, a voyeur. The notes of the piano began slowly and gently. Bruce closed his eyes and let the melody draw him in. Shantel took a deep breath and began to sing.

It only took a moment for your light to shatter my darkness.

Shantel's voice was so clear and beautiful, it gave Terry chills. She looked down at Robby. He was so peaceful. His eyes showed he recognized his mother's voice. She probably played and sang the song often. It was her link to Bobby's heart.

The light of your truth unshackled my mind. I grabbed hold of a forgiveness I never hoped to find. I wasn't even looking; I knew my sins were too black. Before I was born, you carried the cross upon your back. Before my first breath, before my first sin, you died on that cross, my forgiveness to win.

You went to the cross to buy forgiveness for those who could never do it on their own. I was not even good by the standards of men. Yet for me you died, you are the hope for all men. All for forgiveness when none was deserved. Before I was born, my forgiveness reserved.

Terry found herself thinking about the cost of forgiveness. She certainly knew that the church said Jesus died for everyone's sins. She never really felt she did anything that horrible, so she never really pondered it. She just accepted it. She was certainly grateful for it. However, when she looked at it through Bobby's eyes, Chris's eyes, and Bruce's eyes, it put things in a whole different perspective. As the chorus started again, *You went to the cross*—Terry felt tears streaming down her cheeks. Robby was asleep. Karen switched Christine to her shoulder so the baby wouldn't see her crying. Shannon laid claim to the box of tissues on the table. Terry remembered her conversation with Karen. Less than two hours ago, they were talking about forgiveness. It was easy to see how those young men who carried the secret burden of the rape, needed to know that God could not only forgive them, but he could see the better people they would become. No wonder this song made such an impact on them. It was making an impact on her and she didn't feel the same burden of shame they felt. Maybe she should, after all, sin was sin. She saw that Bruce's eyes were still closed as he played, but the tears leaked out just the same. Shantel seemed at peace. Perhaps she was remembering that day when Bobby heard the song for the first time. Terry didn't have any memories like that. What was it like to change someone's life by simply helping them to understand the enormity of grace and forgiveness? On the other hand, what was it like to feel a huge burden lifted off your shoulders by understanding there was hope?

The song came to an end, but no one spoke. Bruce smiled at Shantel, and she put her head on his shoulder. He put his arm around her. It was Shantel who spoke first. "I have no doubt that some of Bobby's friends will be annoyed by that song. First, they don't know the truth of why it meant so much, and second, people hate thinking they need forgiveness. I was afraid of how you three would react, but I can see by the tears, you get it."

"People will be annoyed, why?" Karen asked.

"Most definitely. They don't want to hear all that God stuff. I know some people from Bobby's job won't come to the funeral for that very reason. They couldn't understand why Bobby spent so much time doing things at the church. They burst out laughing when he mentioned Bible study. They thought it was a perfectly useless way to spend a Thursday night."

Terry didn't know what to say. She never made fun of anyone for going to a Bible study, but, then again, did she know anyone who went to a Bible study? She looked at Shannon and knew that Shannon was thinking the same thing she was. *What happens at a Bible study?*

After about two hours, the babies were completely calm and smiley. Bobby's parents seemed rested. It was time to go back home. On the drive back, Bruce said, "You ladies did very, very well. You stayed calm and it helped keep the kiddos calm. I have no doubt that they sense the grief in that house. Babies seem to pick up on emotions."

"That's what my friend in California used to say," Karen agreed. "That's why she tried hard to stay calm when Casey, the baby, was colicky. It's hard to do. You feel so helpless."

"I really didn't do too much," Shannon said. "I was just an extra pair of hands."

"I think that made it easier to stay relaxed," Terry explained. "None of us had to worry about getting something to drink, or finding baby wipes. It really helped, Shannon. You did more than you realize."

"I second that," Bruce said.

As they walked up the walkway to the teahouse, Karen said, "Phew, that was more work than an extremely hectic day at the teahouse. I'm pooped."

"I hear ya," Bruce added. "I was amazed that Bobby and Shantel managed to keep it all together after working all day."

Taking off her coat, Terry turned to Bruce and said, "Speaking of work, any idea about when you can go home?"

"Technically, I can go home any time I want," Bruce said. "But I live in the middle of nowhere. I have a great security system; it's what I do. Still, Greg doesn't think it's safe for me to go home. There's no one around me for a mile or so. If someone did break in, it would take a while for the police to reach me. Greg says he wants more information on the murders before I go home. I have my guys checking my house. We're hoping that whoever was murdering people is done, now that the reunion is over."

"We were just saying you've had one of the worst weeks in history," Karen said.

"It hasn't even been a week. Yeah, I think that's another reason why I like hanging with Greg. I'm not out of the loop, and he knew Bobby and Chris. Actually, I forgot to tell you that Mr. Wiggins hired someone to look into the birth record issue."

"That's good news. The attorney should get to the bottom of things quickly," Karen said. "I noticed you didn't bring it up with Shantel."

"Naw, why bring it up now? When I know something for sure, then I'll tell her. She has enough to deal with at the moment. When we're beyond speculation and rumor, I'll tell her."

Bruce's cell rang again and he answered. "Hi. What––" He frowned, mid-sentence. "But, what would make––" he asked, stopping again. "How the h––"

Terry studied his face. She could hear what sounded like Tom's voice on the other end, but she couldn't make out what he was saying. Bruce was obviously confused. He hung up.

"What?" all three woman asked in unison.

"Thumhart got a warrant to arrest Winston," Bruce said, shaking his head.

"How?" Karen asked.

"Well, Bobby did receive the texts he said, and Coach's phone shows calls. All were made from a throw-away phone. Winston wasn't at the Friday night dinner. He said he was home, but his parents slipped and said he and Anna had gone out. Then, they changed their story and said they were driving around, talking, because of his conflicting feelings about going to the reunion. No one saw them. Combine that with the bartender's story about seeing a woman matching Anna's description walking toward Sandy before the lights went out, and Thumhart has a theory."

"Where's Greg?" Terry asked.

"In someone's office, screaming about the arrest warrant," Bruce said, with a shrug.

"Greenley?" Terry asked.

"Yeah."

No one spoke; they all stared at each other. "Anyone up for a ride?" Bruce asked.

"Why?" Karen queried.

"Because I don't think Coach had any contact whatsoever with Winston Barnstead. I don't think he would know the guy if he tripped over him. I saw yearbooks at Coach's house. I bet, even if I show him a picture, that Coach doesn't know Winston. It's no secret we were blue ribbon jerks in high school, but we really didn't do anything that horrible to Winston. There are plenty of people for him to hate worse than us. Winston had reason to dislike us, no doubt, but kill us, no. I want to see if Coach remembers anything relevant. Maybe Coach did have contact with him. Maybe Coach gave Winston reason to hate us. The only one who can tell us is Coach. I'm sticking with my theory that Coach won't even recognize Winston from the yearbook."

"I'll go," Karen said. I'm starting to get my second win.

"You both go," Shannon said. "I need to help my mom get some things done at home."

"Okay, see you tomorrow, "Terry said, as she and Karen headed out the door behind Bruce. Terry was exhausted, but she wasn't going to miss this. She was hoping, like Karen, she got a second wind.

CHAPTER 18

As they pulled up to Coach's house, Bruce said, "I gotta warn you, it's a mess in there. He's emotionally falling apart. His car is here, so he must be home." They went up the walk. The screen door was shut, but the front door was slightly ajar. Bruce knocked on the screen. When there was no answer, he tried the screen door. It was locked. "Coach, it's Bruce. Open up." There was a shuffling inside. Bruce knocked again. "Hey, buddy, it's cold out here. Open up, it's important." A creaking came from the back of the house. "He's probably throwing his garbage out the back door. Hold on, I'll go help him and let you ladies in. Hang tight. I'll make it fast."

Terry watched as Bruce trudged around the side of the house. "I hope this helps," Terry said to Karen. "I really don't think Winst—" She was cut off by a yell from the back. She and Karen raced around to the backyard. As Terry came around the side corner, she saw a man vault over a fence. He wore a bulky, black coat and a black hat, or maybe it was a ski mask. Bruce was running behind him, and cleared the fence with one jump.

"Dang," said Karen.

"Coach!" yelled Terry. She ran up the back steps and yanked open the heavy metal all-weather door. She ran into the kitchen with Karen right behind her. She reached the living room and saw Coach's feet dangling over the arm of couch. Papers, clothes and garbage were everywhere.

"Coach, my gosh, are you—" she stopped. There was no need for her to ask if he was okay. She saw Coach's lifeless eyes staring at her. There was a bullet hole in his head, and black feathers on his body.

The front screen door rattled. Terry heard Bruce yell, "It's me, Bruce." She opened the screen door for him. Before she could speak, Bruce saw Coach. "I was afraid of this," he said. "I lost the guy, but not before he dropped this," Bruce said as he held up a gun in his gloved hand.

"Oh, no, you shouldn't touch that," Karen wailed.

"I was not leaving it on the sidewalk for him to come back and get. I called 911. They should be here–" He stopped as Karen pushed Terry out of the way and bolted through the kitchen. Terry followed her. Karen slammed the back door open and threw up over the iron railing on the back steps. *My thoughts, exactly*, thought Terry.

***

"Okay, let's take it from the top," Officer Andrew Burdick said. Terry, Bruce and Karen were all huddled in Coach's driveway. Police and dogs were all over the place. While waiting for the police to get there, Bruce called Greg, and Karen called Henry. The three of them were now explaining for the third time why they were there. Terry liked Officer Burdick. His voice was deep and soothing. She knew Greg liked him, too. She heard Greg say a few times, "Thank God, Burdick was there." If it couldn't be Greg or Tom, Burdick was the best port in the storm.

"I said get out of my way and you better do it now," a nasally voice barked. A tall man Terry didn't recognize came storming up the driveway.

"Detective Thumhart," Burdick said, nodding.

Thumhart ignored him. He looked at Terry, Bruce and Karen and said, "You three were butting in, why?"

Terry wanted to say, *because you're an incompetent ass*, but knew that would not help the situation.

Bruce stood up straight, took a step forward, and said, "Excuse me, Detective, but I fail to see what makes you think we were butting into anything. We've told the officers that we came to check up on Coach. I heard the back door and came around the back in time to see a man running across the snow there. What makes that butting in?"

Thumhart sneered. "Oh, you don't fool me. I know exactly who you are. You're Mullin's little troop of friends. Playing detective, were you?"

"I believe it's you who likes to *play* detective," Bruce snarled.

Uh-oh, thought Terry. *This can't be good.*

"Don't think I won't have the three of you thrown in jail for interfering with an investigation."

"Do you expect us to believe that line of drivel?" Karen asked. "Because we aren't interfering with anything. We can visit anyone we want."

"Listen here, girly," Thumhart started.

"Let's just back that truck up, Jack. Did you just refer to me as *girly?*"

And, heeere we go, Terry thought. *Oh, buddy, you just made the biggest mistake of your life.*

"Did he just call me girly?" Karen asked Bruce.

"Yeah, I distinctively heard *girly*," Bruce said. "What about you, Terry?"

There was no way to remain neutral. She might as well throw her hat into the ring. "Yuppers. Clear as a bell. I heard *girly*."

"Detective, who is your supervisor?"

Thumhart was not having it. He was in full bully mode, and it was clear there was no backing down now. "Don't get uppity with me, missy."

Terry knew her eyes went wide. Even Officer Burdick took a step backward.

"Who in the world do you honestly think—" Karen started.

"That'll be enough," another officer in a State Police uniform said as he walked up the driveway toward them. He was at least Thumhart's height with a buzz cut. The man was kind-looking, but seemed to have the words "in charge" written all over him. Greg was right behind him.

"Captain Greenley," Thumhart said.

Ooooo, you's in big trouble, Terry thought. It was very hard to keep from grinning.

"Officer?" The man nodded at Burdick.

"Burdick, sir."

"Officer Burdick, have these nice people already given their statements?"

"Yes, sir. I was just about to go over them."

"Good man. Please take them to your cruiser and finish, if that's agreeable with you. It's quite cold out here. Those poor women's lips are blue. I believe the gentleman at the end of the driveway there—" Greenley nodded toward Henry.

"Mr. Sanders, sir," Greg added.

"Yes, quite right. I believe Mr. Sanders can take them home when you're finished."

"Right, sir." Officer Burdick began to usher them down the driveway.

"But I'm not done," Thumhart said.

"Oh, yes, you are," Captain Greenley replied.

It was all Terry could do to not turn around and stick out her tongue.

CHAPTER 19

Terry was amazed; it was six p.m. and the teahouse tables were brimming with potluck casseroles, salads and desserts. No one, it seemed, wanted to be left out when it came to hearing about their afternoon. When Uncle Henry pulled up to the teahouse, Aunt Rose and the Dindles were on them like bubble gum in a kid's hair. Mr. Wiggins, having heard about it on the news, called Henry's cell phone, and Henry filled Sam in. That's when Rose and Mrs. Dindle went into organization mode. Cell phones were brought out, calls were made, and, voila, a dinner was arranged, complete with the Wiggins and the Fair Meadows scoop patrol. Once they knew Hattie Mullins was coming, it only made sense to invite Greg's mother and sister, Anna. Unfortunately, it was the night of their bowling league party. Hattie promised to fill them in. Also missing would be Tom and Shannon. Tom volunteered to stay back at the station and keep an ear out and Shannon was taking dinner over to him. Thankfully, Walter Nissan volunteered to drive the scoop patrol. Terry would have preferred a few hours of peace and quiet, but she acquiesced to the dinner. She didn't want to disappoint Aunt Rose.

"God bless Henry," Karen said.

"Yeah, he's a rock," Terry said. "He told me that Rose is having a tough time after what happened. Who wouldn't? They're going to stay at the hotel tonight, again. Henry is hoping it will help Rose relax. I can't believe him. He was the one in the hospital and he's worried about her."

"He's probably worried about her because she's hovering over him," Karen said. "If he doesn't distract her, she most likely focuses on fussing over him. Poor guy is probably staying at the hotel because he wants a break."

"They really do complement each other perfectly," Bruce observed. "I find it funny, the way Henry can get Rose to do something his way, and vice versa."

Terry chuckled. "Yeah, it's funny as long as they aren't doing it at the same time. When they have opposite goals in mind, look out. It's fireworks time in Maine."

"Does it happen often?" Bruce asked.

"No, not really," Karen said. "Uncle Henry's pretty laid back. Aunt Rose is the kind of person who loves a good crisis. It brings out the best in her. Did you see how expertly she organized tonight? I guarantee you, by the time people leave here tonight, things will be clean and ready for us tomorrow, and no one will have done too much or too little. It's her gift."

Karen's face became serious. "Bruce, you know the Wiggins are coming tonight. Can you handle that?"

"Yeah, I was furious at first that they didn't tell me that Matthew looks like me, and is probably my son. However, my mother reminded me that they didn't know until this weekend. Also, I raped Donna. Maybe we shouldn't tell Matthew for a while. I can't be mad. I was the one in the wrong all those years ago. I called Mr. Wiggins. We're going to let things settle for a bit. It's hard for them. Matthew is their world. It's why Rachelle left town so quickly after the reunion. She didn't want to risk anyone running into Matthew." Bruce ran his fingers through his dark curly hair. He looked back at Karen and shrugged. "It'll all work out."

"Man, these past few days must seem like a lifetime to you," Terry said. She couldn't imagine what Bruce must be going through, his whole life was suddenly different. His two closest friends and his high school coach were murdered; he confessed to a rape, he was also probably being hunted down; and it turned out he had a son.

"Do you think any of it has really sunk in?" Karen asked. "It's a lot to handle."

"No, I'm sure it hasn't sunk in. This afternoon at Bobby's parents' house was surreal. I said the words that Bobby and Chris are gone, but I don't think I really believe it yet. It's like I expect this to all be a dream. I just keep going. It's all I can do, for now."

"Yeah, I guess you're right," Karen said.

The Wiggins walked in. Sam and Bruce nodded to each other.

"I'm gonna go say hello," Bruce said. He stood and walked over to Sam and Sarah.

Terry could tell by Sarah's downcast eyes and Sam's cautions eyes, that it was an awkward moment. "I give Bruce a ton of credit," she said to Karen. "He's handling this mess with courage and humility. Shantel put everything in perspective for me this afternoon. How about you?"

Karen shrugged, her face a bit sad. "Yes, but I don't think it matters. When I saw Bruce with Shantel, I realized that he belongs with her. They share a past. He loves those babies. I was trying really hard not to feel much for him. Still, I felt a twinge of jealousy this afternoon. It's stupid, I know."

"No, it's not stupid. Just remember that Shantel just lost Bobby. Who knows what will happen."

"Oh, I know that. I'm just saying that I want to keep my emotional distance at the moment. It's a weird and complicated situation."

"No kidding. I don't think any of us has a grip on what has happened since Friday. It's craziness."

The tables were arranged to make a large rectangle. The food was making its way around. The three stars had their chance to tell their story.

"Did the man look familiar at all?" Dottie Dindle asked Bruce.

"I never saw his face. He was wearing a ski mask. Whoever it is, he's in great shape."

"You're no slouch," Karen said. "You went over that fence with ease."

"It's the hurdle training from high school. I stop by the high school near me and help out the sports coaches now and again. I really like working with the kids. Honestly, though, it was probably adrenaline. I thought the guy was robbing Coach. It wasn't until I started to jog back and I saw the gun that I started to think about Coach being killed."

"Any chance it was someone from our track team?" Greg asked.

"I couldn't say," Bruce answered. "I've racked my brain over and over. Nothing about his body, his gait, or his clothes looked familiar."

"Girls, how awful it must have been to discover Coach like that," Hattie Mullins said.

"I'm honestly surprised that I wasn't sick alongside Karen," Terry answered.

"What happened after we left?" Bruce asked Greg.

"Well, since Winston Barnstead was in police custody, and his wife was in the police station ready to post bail, he was let go with no bail and the charges are dropped."

"And that windbag Thumhart?" Bruce continued.

"Unfortunately, he's still working the case. The only change is that he takes his cues from me. He's pretty ticked off. He's not allowed to question anyone without me there. Greenley called him a rude buffoon," Greg said, chuckling. "Personally, I would've liked to watch Karen take him apart, but it just wasn't to be." Greg laughed out loud and said, "Greenley told Thumhart, 'Young man, no wonder you aren't married. You don't talk to a lady like that, and I can tell, that one there's a spitfire. If I hadn't showed up when I did, she'd have had your badge on a platter, right next to your head. Not only are you a rude buffoon, but I'm starting to think you might be just plain stupid!' Thumhart turned six shades of purple."

It was quiet for a few beats. Then, Sam Wiggins cleared his throat. "I want to let you all know that the attorney I spoke with today called me back about an hour ago. Donna had two babies. Matthew and a girl named," his voice caught, "Sarah. Donna left the hospital with both of them. There is no record of the girl being put up for adoption."

"Oh, no," Bruce said. "Could that baby have been in the car with Donna?" His voice cracked. His eye looked panicked.

"That was my initial fear, but I don't see how. The front of the car was the part that burned the worst. Nothing was really left of the front, but the car split in two. If there was a car seat in the back, I think they would have found it, and the body."

"I do so wish we could remember the name of that woman who brought us Matthew," Sarah Wiggins said.

"I know her name," Katie Wiggins said.

"You do?" Sarah asked. "How could you possibly remember her name?"

"It's easy. Her name was Denise Frenchion. I remember thinking it ironic that her last name had French in it and she lived by the Canadian border."

"My gosh, Mother," Sam Wiggins said. "You may have just saved the day."

"Why didn't you tell us?" Sarah Wiggins asked.

"No one ever asked me," Katie said, incredulously. "How was I to know my memory was superior to yours, my dear?"

"Do you think we can find her?" Sarah Wiggins asked, her hand reaching out and grabbing Sam's arm.

"Maybe she's still in Maine," Bruce added.

"When we wanted to find some people from high school whose families weren't around, we used the internet," Terry explained excitedly.

"We got quite good at it," Karen chimed in.

"You can always start with the address on the birth certificate," Bruce added.

"I suppose if that doesn't work, I can hire a private investigator," Sam said.

"I want to try and find her without a private investigator," Sarah said. "A private investigator might take too long. What if he tips her off we're looking for her? I don't want to give her a chance to run," Sarah added breathlessly.

Rose perked up. "Let's go check it out ourselves!"

"Oh, yes! What a wonderful idea!" Sarah Wiggins exclaimed. "Can we go tomorrow?"

"Well, I'm not sure about tomorrow," Henry said, but he was not allowed to finish his thought.

"I think we should go back to the hotel, have a few drinks, and plan a strategy," Rose chimed in.

"Marvelous idea," Maude said, leaning forward in her seat. "Don't you agree, Walter?"

"Well," Walter considered a moment, eying Henry. "I'm always up for a road trip. It does take the boredom out of things."

"So, we're on?" Rose asked. Terry wanted to laugh. Rose looked like a child who'd just learned she was going to Disney World.

"Now, everyone just hold on one second," Henry barked.

"What in the world for?" Rose asked.

Terry realized she was a bit dizzy from watching the exchange. It was all happening so fast, it was like watching a cartoon episode of Ricochet Rabbit.

"How are you all going to get there?" Henry asked.

"Rent a van," Walter explained. "I suggest those of us who want to embark on this little venture book rooms at the hotel. We can plan tonight and leave first thing in the morning. It will save time by omitting the driving back and forth."

"Oh, my goodness, this is all so exciting," Sarah exclaimed, clapping her hands.

"Dottie," Rose said, jumping up. "You have to come, too. We'll gladly pay for the room. Don't worry about any of that."

"Hmmmm, well—I—um."

Terry knew Mrs. Dindle was not about to put Henry on the hook for her room.

"Oh, for heaven's sake, Dottie," Henry barked. "Just say you'll go. If you don't, Rose will fuss all night."

Dottie looked at Rose, who was nodding vigorously. "Okay, I guess I'm in," she giggled. "I better call Shannon."

"I can't believe this is happening," Karen said. "I'm with Henry on this one. I'm not so sure this is a good idea."

Rose waved her off. "Quit being a spoiled sport. I, for one, am not getting any younger. A little adventure on a lark gives me a boost and puts some pep in my step. Besides, this is about the only chance this ol' gal is gonna have to throw a party in a hot tub. You should see the beauties the hotel brought in to make up for the pool being out of commission."

Sam Wiggins cleared his throat. "Sorry to be a party pooper, but I'm not staying at a hotel. I like my own bed. I'll drop Sarah off if you want to continue this. I have the address you need. I think it's a little too last minute, but you might discover something. I'll even buy the gas."

Terry saw Henry open his mouth to speak. Rose glowered at him and he shut it. Terry looked at Greg. He was frowning.

"Well, I suppose if you're going to go through with this, I'll drive Bruce and the girls over to the hotel. We'll help you plan. I'll call Tom. He and Shannon can meet us there." He shook his head. "You all go on ahead. The girls and I will clean up here and meet you there."

Rose jumped up, threw her arms around Greg and gave him a kiss on the cheek. "This will be fun. I know we're throwing caution to the wind, but I gotta say again, 'why not live a little?' I'm excited."

Terry didn't know what to say. She shrugged and got up to help put things away. It was going to be a long night and she was already exhausted. She wasn't sure if she wanted to cheer Rose on or slap her silly.

***

Terry, Karen and Shannon walked into the bar with Greg, Tom and Bruce in tow. It was unsettling to be back in the hotel. Just a few days ago— Terry looked around. It felt odd to be looking for Uncle Henry and Aunt Rose in a bar, let alone the rest of the elderly members of the scoop patrol. There was the mild thump, thump, thump of the bass from the music overhead. The highly polished dark wood bar with black edging radiated a warm glow. The golden square and circle design on the front panels brought out the shine of the wood. The male and female bartenders in their black shirts and white aprons were zipping from place to place. Terry was surprised how busy the place was. Terry recognized one of the bartenders from the night of the black-out. The woman nodded to them and smiled.

"Hellooooo, yoohooo," came a call from the far end of the bar. Rose was waving away.

"Holy macaroni," Karen whispered. "I think ol' Rosey's had a few."

"Yeah, well, look at good ol' Dottie sitting right up there next to her," Shannon added. "We better go find out what the heck they're drinking. This can't, I repeat, can't be good."

"Is it my imagination, or is Rosey glowing," Greg whispered from behind.

Terry held up her hand. "I can't think about it. Cover us, we're goin' in," she said.

"Girls," snapped Rose, as they approached. "Why did you never share the news about butterscotch schnapps? This wonderful bartender shared the news of—what was it, dear?"

"A caramel apple shot," the bartender said with a smile.

"Yeah, that."

"Rosey, there you are," Henry said, coming up with Maude and Walter. "The rooms are all set. Walter even hired a car for tomorrow."

"We even found a map in the gift shop," Walter added.

"The van comes with a GPS," Maude said.

"Never trust those evil things," Walter retorted. "Damn near wound up in a lake, a few years ago. Give me a good old map any day."

"Well," chirped Rose, weaving a bit, "we discovered butterscotch schnapps."

"Rose, Dottie, you two don't really drink," Henry said, shocked. "I've only been gone about half an hour."

"Well," Maude said, eyebrows up and a smirk on her face, "there have been other drinking occasions. There was the Boone's Farm Strawberry Wine incident of '72."

"Was my mother in on that one?" Shannon asked.

"Hell, yeah," insisted Dottie Dindle. "And the blackberry brandy incident of '64."

Rose and Dottie howled with laughter. Henry and companions chuckled. Terry shot a glance at her friends. Greg, Bruce and Tom all had their hands over their mouths, eyes cast downward. They were shaking with laughter. Karen and Shannon, like her, were stunned.

"Oh, yeah, and the bridge club wine tasting incident sometime in the 80's." Maude chuckled.

"Oh, yeah, now that was a good time." Rose nodded.

"Rose, we were planning on going in the hot tubs," Henry snapped.

"Oh, baby, I'm still okay to hop in the hot tub!" Rose said, sliding off the bar stool. "Which room are we in?"

"We're in 132, right off the pool, and Dottie is right next door in 134."

"You're *really* gonna get in a hot tub?" Karen asked incredulously. "I don't think it's a good idea when you've been drinking."

"Relax," said Rose. "Dottie and I only had a shot."

"Or two," added Dottie.

"Or three," added Rose, walking away, holding on to Henry. Dottie was holding on to Rose.

"Oh, Lord," whispered Shannon.

"If we're gonna stay here, might as well have some fun," Maude said, shrugging.

"I agree," shouted Rose over her shoulder, and, to Terry's horror, she gave Henry's left butt cheek a squeeze.

"I'm gonna puke," Karen said.

"I think I'm going blind," Terry added. She turned around as an odd sound caught her attention.

Greg, Bruce and Tom were doubled over, holding on to the bar, laughing. Terry looked at the bartender who smiled and winked.

Karen leaned over to the bartender. "I know you usually don't allow non-guests to have a drink by the pool, or hot tubs, in this case, but can you please make an exception?"

The bartender nodded. "I think that would be fine," she cleared her throat, "under the circumstances. They came in and said they wanted a 'desserty type drink.' I gave them a few choices, and they picked that one. It's actually butterscotch schnapps and a shot of apple schnapps."

"It's *two* shots? Oh, good gravy," Shannon howled, putting her head in her hands.

"Okay, everybody order up," Bruce said, stepping up to the bar. "Let's get our drinks and get out there. I'll just have a coke," he said. "I'll be lifeguard on duty."

Terry watched Karen turn to him. She gave him a long look. "You're one heck of a good sport. After what you went through over in that area a few nights ago? I couldn't. I just couldn't."

"It's okay." Bruce held up a hand. "Let's just not talk about it. We gotta get out there. I think it'll actually be interesting. Your aunt is a riot."

"More than we ever knew," Karen said. "More than we ever knew."

They settled down at a table near an empty hot tub. There were a number of other guests in the other hot tubs. Dottie, Rose and Maude got right in. Terry smiled.

The ladies were having the time of their lives. Henry and Walter joined them at the table. Henry was shaking his head.

"Rose is pretty well lit up," he said.

"Ya, think?" Karen asked. "Now, Terry and I want to know who was taking care of us during the drinking incidents mentioned earlier at the bar? Was my mom involved in things like the Boone's Farm incident of '72?"

"Oh, sure," Henry said. "Madeline never missed out. Your dad and I were relegated to babysitting. Some, of course, were before you were born. Tucker Dindle was usually with us. You girls played. It was just a sleepover for you. Eventually, one of us would go get the women and roll them into the car." He chuckled. "Those are some fun memories," he said. "Not too many left, I'm afraid. I guess I'm glad Rose pushed the issue on this one."

Bruce raised his glass. "Here's to pushing the issue!"

"Hear! Hear! HEAR! HEAR!" they all chorused.

Greg's cell rang. He took it out and looked at it. "Now what?" he asked as he answered. "Mullins. Hey, Andrew." It seemed to Terry that no one was breathing. "Really, are you sure? You're going over there? Want back-up? Okay, call me later."

He looked around the table. "Okay, I'm not supposed to tell you, so—"

"We promise," Henry cut in. Everyone nodded and crossed their hearts in unison.

"The gun that killed Coach and Chris is registered to Adam Weaver's father. Burdick is on his way over to talk to them."

"Adam Weaver? Donna's friend?" Henry asked.

Greg nodded.

Silence filled the room until Henry whispered, "Oh, holy mother of pearl!"

CHAPTER 20

"Are you really sure you don't want to go, and I'll stay here and help Shannon?" Terry asked Karen.

"I'm quite positive. There's no way I want to spend six hours, one way, mind you, in a car with Aunt Rose, Mrs. Dindle, Sarah Wiggins, Maude Despard, and Mr. Nissan. I don't care if they are renting a minivan. Regardless of Aunt Rose packing the picnic basket, I'd rather stay here. I honestly hope you find that woman. I think it's a great sign that the last known address for Denise Frenchion that Uncle Henry and Mr. Wiggins found online last night is the same address on the birth certificate. Hopefully, they'll find more helpful information online today."

A horn beeped in the driveway. "Well, here I go. It's four a.m. and I'm off in a minivan full of seniors."

"Best of luck, little sister!"

Terry climbed in the front seat, next to Mr. Nissan. "No one else wants to sit up front?" she asked.

"We figured your eyesight is better than ours, so it made sense for you to be the navigator, dear," Aunt Rose explained.

"I have a thermos of coffee and some cups if anyone wants some," Terry said.

Mr. Nissan glared at her. "I already told 'em, I'm only making three potty stops. I'm not making a six hour trip into nine."

"Okay, got it," Terry said. *Oh, isn't this gonna be a blast,* she thought.

The other women mostly napped and Terry kept Walter Nissan company and periodically checked the map. It agreed with the GPS in the rental car, but Mr. Nissan was not going to trust the GPS system. No way, no how. He had the radio station on and was cheerfully singing along with the songs of the fifties and sixties. By nine o'clock, everyone was awake and Terry listened to the fifties and sixties music on the radio as they all sang along. sing-along. *Three potty-stops or not,* thought Terry. *I need every cup of coffee I can get!* She refilled her cup to Dion's *The Wanderer.*

After the ten o'clock rest stop break, which was their third and last allowed stop, Mr. Nissan reached into a small lunch box type bag. "I got us a treat, ladies," he said. "Nothing says Christmas time road trip like this." He took out a CD and gave it to Terry to put into the CD player.

She looked down at it. *Bing Crosby, Dean Martin, Frank Sinatra and Your Other Favorites Croon the Christmas Classics.* Terry pondered the idea of getting out and walking. Instead she decided to just go with it.

An hour later, they pulled up in front of a small yellow house with black shutters. It was in a neighborhood that was, Terry guessed, built in the 1950s. "Well, what now?" Walter Nissan asked.

"We go ask questions," said Rose, wiggling out of the passenger side. It was obvious she was stiff, but she marched right up the walk. She was a woman on a mission. Terry scooted out after her. Rose went right up to the door and began to knock. Everyone else was still trying to get out of the van. They tumbled out and scurried up the front walk.

A young man opened the front door. "Can I help you folks?"

"Well, we're trying to locate someone who was living in this house about twenty years ago," Rose volunteered.

"Twenty years? Wow, that's a long time ago. People come and go out of this neighborhood fairly often. I've only lived in this house about two years. You could try Mrs. Becket, next door. She's lived here her whole life. If anyone could help you, it's her."

En masse, they trudged next door. Rose rang the doorbell. There was some shuffling, and an elderly face peered out the window. A short while later, the door front door opened a crack. "May I help you?" said a very small, shaky voice.

This time, Sarah Wiggins spoke up. "We're trying to locate a friend of my daughter's," she explained. "The woman's name was Denise Frenchion. We think she lived here about twenty years ago. The man next door thought you might be able to help us."

The woman opened the door and stared at them. Terry assumed she was trying to figure out if this patrol of seniors, and one young whippersnapper, were dangerous. "Well, I guess you all might as well come in. Twenty years is a long time. I'm gonna have to think on this."

They trooped into the woman's home. It was beautiful. Terry realized right away that the woman had made every slipcover, every cushion, every doily, and every quilt. The furniture probably belonged to the woman's parents. "You did all of this, didn't you?" Terry asked.

"Well, me and Larry, God rest his soul. There wasn't any piece of furniture that Larry and I couldn't make good as new. My son has the business now. He's as talented as my Larry was. I was a whiz at the sewing machine. Still do some quilting. Much slower than I used to be, but it keeps me busy. My name is Bernice. Bernice Becket."

In turn, they all introduced themselves.

"Now who was it you were asking about?"

"Denise Frenchion," Sarah answered.

"Well, you all have a seat now. Can I get you some tea? Got the kettle on, it's no trouble."

When everyone was seated and the tea politely declined, the woman took out a photo album and began looking through it. "Now, that name does sound quite familiar. Although, I don't remember a Denise next door. Let me think." She started at the front and slowly went through the album, page by painstaking page. "This here woman's name was Bertha Frenchion. Her husband Fred passed on early. Bertha died when her kids were just about grown. She had three children. What were their names?"

"Was one Denise?" Rose prompted.

"No, no, that's what has me confused. There was a boy named Arnold, a girl named Marion, and a younger sister. Now, maybe that youngest one was Denise. That one was no good, got into drugs. Let me see. There must be a picture here somewhere. We used to have summer barbeques all the time."

Everyone sat stock still as the woman looked at pages and mumbled and chuckled to herself. "Now, here's something. See, this woman is Bertha. These are the kids."

Sarah Wiggins just about dove on the couch and seated herself next to the woman. She peered at the photograph. She frowned. "Maybe, this girl here. Is that Denise?"

"No, that would be Marion. She was a nurse. She and her brother took care of the mother when she got sick. Stayed on for a bit after she died. Then they sold the house and moved on."

"Do you remember her having a friend with children?" Maude Despard asked.

"Now that you mention it, I do. After the mother passed, a young pregnant girl came to stay with them. Very quiet girl. Arnold loved her something fierce. I remember he doted on her and her kids, once she had 'em."

"Was this the girl?" Sarah Wiggins asked, pulling out her wallet and showing the woman Donna's high school picture."

"Yes!" said Bernice. "Yes, that was her. Sweet girl. Awful sad, she was. Cried a lot, as I recall. What was her name? It's right on the tip of my tongue."

"Donna," Terry suggested, hopefully.

"Why, yes, yes, it was. Poor thing died in a car crash, as I remember. I didn't know a thing about it. One day, I saw Arnold and asked about her and he mumbled about her being gone."

Terry watched as the woman looked out the window. She was obviously thinking, lost in the past.

"Now I remember who Denise was. She was the younger sister. I remember them yelling and fighting over there when she came to stay there. Marion told me they were trying to get her some help for her drug addiction. If the girl wasn't high, she was drunk. I think that Donna's death set her right, though. When that girl died, all the fighting stopped. Never saw Denise at all after that. Arnold said she couldn't bear to come outside, she was just too sick. She pretty much kept to the house."

"What do you remember about Donna's children?"

"Now that was the funny thing about it. After Donna died, the boy went to live with his father. The girl stayed with them. Why the father only took the—"

"They kept the girl?" everyone asked in unison.

"Yes, isn't that what I just said? The father didn't want her. Arnold cried for days after the little boy left. I'm sure he was sick to death over losing Donna, too."

"Where did they move?" Walter Nissan asked.

"No idea. One day, they were just gone. A few months later, the house sold. That's all I know."

"Could I take another look at those pictures?" Sarah asked.

"Oh, honey, just take what you want. I got no use for 'em. I have bladder cancer. I'm going in for surgery next week. I won't be around much longer. I'll help you. You can take all the pictures of the Frenchions. You knew Donna?" she asked Sarah. "I think you must be her mother 'cause she looked just like you," Bernice Becket said.

Sarah nodded. "Yes, Donna was my daughter."

"Why are you looking for Denise after all these years?"

"She has my granddaughter," Sarah said. "It's a very long story. That little girl they kept is my granddaughter, and we just found out about her. Now we want to find her."

"Just found out about her! What a terrible shame!" Bernice exclaimed. "If you want to find that little girl, you find Arnold. He'll know where she is. She was everything to him."

"You have no idea where they might have gone?" Sarah asked. Terry could see that the woman's heart was breaking.

"Sorry, no. You might want to try the local high school. They might know who you can ask, on the count of reunions and things like that. Every once in a while, I see notices in the church bulletins about people they want to try and locate for one thing or another. That's another place you might want to try. I believe the family went to the local Methodist church. It's on

Main Street. Can't miss it. I wish I could be more help to all of you. Do you have a number? I probably won't remember anything, but if I do, I'll let you know."

Sarah Wiggins pulled out a business card. "This is my husband. Please call him if you remember anything at all, even if it seems small. You never know."

They thanked Mrs. Becket for everything. They wished her well with her upcoming surgery. Terry was hoping the woman would remember something. The group loaded themselves back into the van.

"Okay, ladies, where to now? High school? Church?"

"I don't know," Sarah wailed.

"Don't give up hope," Maude admonished. "We've only just started the search."

"She might call with more information," Mrs. Dindle said.

"I say we go to the church," Rose said, matter-of-factly. "I know what Shannon and Karen went through to locate people. I'm not holding out much hope for the high school, but the church might have something."

"I agree with Aunt Rose," Terry said. "Karen and Shannon had to jump through hoops to find some of our classmates. The local churches had some addresses from the parents. The parents still kept in touch with friends in town. Let's head to the church."

Mrs. Becket was correct; there was no way to miss the large brick building with the steeple. It also had a sign that gave the hours for services.

"Do you want me to run in and ask?" Terry queried. "It's easiest for me to get out."

"No, I need to go in. I have too much nervous energy," Sarah Wiggins said.

Terry understood, but it meant getting Aunt Rose and Mrs. Dindle out. They really hadn't planned the seating well for this short trip. Terry climbed out and opened the sliding door to the passenger side. Mrs. Dindle got out with a few pppffffft noises. Rose's eyes opened wide since she happened to be about eye level with Dottie's backside. Terry thought how sad it was that Uncle Henry missed it. He would have chuckled about it for days. Telling him about it wouldn't have the same impact. Mr. Nissan did turn and raise an eyebrow. Aunt Rose climbed out and Terry tipped the passenger seat in the middle row forward allowing Mrs. Wiggins to climb out. The women stared at each other for a second or two.

"Well, we might was well all go in," Rose said. "It sure beats climbing in and out yet another time once you come out."

"Maude and I can hold down the fort until you get back," Mr. Nissan said.

"Okay, but no necking in the back seat," Rose admonished.

"You're just jealous," Maude Despard said.

"Maybe," Rose said.

"Enough, enough, enough," Terry said. "Not in front of the child!" Everyone laughed, but Terry still shuddered as she thought of Rose grabbing Henry's butt. *I just can't deal with the thought of old people sex,* she thought.

Terry held the door for the three other women. They trooped in and found the office. "Can I help you ladies?" the middle-aged woman behind the desk asked. She was perfectly coiffed and wore a stunning blue and white pantsuit. Her big brown eyes reminded Terry of a deer. Her red fingernails sported little green wreaths.

"We're hoping you can help us find someone," Sarah explained. "We're trying to locate a family with the last name of Frenchion. A Mrs. Becket said you might have an address for them."

"Bernice Becket?" the church secretary asked.

Terry nodded along with the other three women. "We just spoke to her," Terry explained. "That led us to you."

"Yes, we know Mrs. Becket; she is such a dear," the woman with the red nails said. "She comes here often for our church suppers. The seniors love our suppers. Hmmm, any particular reason you want to find the Frenchions?" the woman asked.

Terry felt a rush of hope. She said Frenchion like she knew them. Maybe she did. Maybe they were nearby.

"They were friends of my daughter's," Sarah explained. "She died in a car accident years ago, but we're hoping they can give us more information. She lived with the Frenchions."

The blue pantsuited woman studied them carefully. "I really can't give out any information. That's private," she said.

Terry noticed Sarah's eyes grow wide with panic. "Well, well, is there a minister here who we might talk to?"

That was it. Blue pantsuit was not going to have someone going over her head. "No, not today. He'll be back tomorrow afternoon. Do you have a card or can you give me a number to reach you?"

Sarah's eyes filled with tears. She reached in her purse and took out one of Mr. Wiggin's business cards, along with tissues. She handed the woman the card.

Terry saw Rose straighten up. Uh oh, Rose's ire was up. You shouldn't make Rosie's friends cry. Karen came by her pluck honestly.

"You know," Rose said, her words clipped. "We came here for help. We thought the church would be the place to go. We obviously aren't criminals. Really, how fast could I possibly run? I suppose I could dye my hair white to look older, but you can't fake wrinkles like this," she said, rolling up her sleeves. "This poor woman lost her granddaughter. Arnold Frenchion and his sisters are the only lead we have. If you know any of them, have them call that number!" She turned and walked out of the church office. Terry, Mrs. Dindle and Sarah Wiggins looked bug-eyed at each other and scurried off behind her. The pantsuited woman, mouth agape, watched them go.

After they regrouped in the van, Mr. Nissan again asked, "Where to now?"

"I'm actually rather hungry," Maude Despard said.

"Me, too," came a chorus of women's voices.

"Well, I spotted a diner a few miles outside of town," Mr. Nissan said. "How does that sound?"

They all agreed.

"Wow, this place is packed," Terry commented, entering the small diner. "Maybe we should try to go somewhere else."

Just then, a hostess returned to the small stand at the entrance. "How many?" she asked.

"Well, there's six of us," Terry said. "We're pretty tired. How long is the wait?"

The hostess turned around. It appeared a group of eight was just getting ready to leave. "You're in luck," the hostess said, smiling. "You came at just the right time. Give us about five minutes. Is that okay?"

Terry turned and looked at the group.

"Wonderful," Rose said.

Terry looked around. She was in love. The diner had a white and black checkered floor, red and chrome seats at the counter, and booths with red seats. Over the counter was a big white sign with red lettering that read Nannie's Place. Terry couldn't be sure, but she was guessing that Nannie was the buxom grey-haired woman who put an order up and yelled something. Waitresses in teal dresses with white aprons and sneakers buzzed about. The waiters were all in white with black bow ties. Terry turned slightly and realized there was now a line of at least ten people behind them.

"Apparently, we came at the perfect time," Terry said. The group turned in unison and nodded.

"Food must be great to attract this type of crowd on a weekday," Walter said.

"Right this way," the hostess said. She was a tall bleached blonde in a long-sleeve white blouse and black pants. Terry noticed she bore a striking resemblance to the woman calling out orders.

"Are you always this packed?" Terry asked.

"Ever since the day my parents opened this place thirty years ago. That's my mother over there," she said, pointing to the grey-haired woman. She handed them all menus.

Immediately, a waitress was at the table with water. As that waitress left, another one stepped up to ask, "Can I offer you folks a drink while you take a look at the menu?"

Drinks were ordered, and Terry began to contemplate the menu. Nannie's offered a different homemade soup every day, along with sandwiches, burgers, salads and a whole page of specials for that day.

"I haven't been to a place like this in years and years," Mrs. Dindle said. "It reminds me of the place that used to be right on the main drag by the gas station."

"You're right," Maude agreed. "That place was always packed like this one. I was crushed when the Whitfields sold it and moved to Florida. What was it called?"

"The Maine Attraction," Walter said. "They tore it down and put up the dress shop that closed. What is it now?"

"Nothing at the moment," Terry said. "There's talk it might become a bookstore."

They all sat quietly, trying to decide what to order. Terry quickly selected the chowder. It seemed like a nice warming, comforting choice. She watched as a few people left and a few others were seated. It was obvious that most were regulars. People waved to each other and called out greetings.

After the orders were given, Walter said, "Well, Sarah, what do you think about what we learned?"

Sarah's eyes filled with tears again. "I'm afraid that either the crazy sister took one of the babies, or they kept one. I think they kept one and fled," she said.

"Do you think Sam will want to hire a private investigator?" Rose asked. "I would, if it was my grandchild."

"He might." Sarah sighed. "There's a part of me that wants to track them down to the ends of the earth. There's another part that just wants to let it go. Who knows what the child, well, young adult at this point, thinks? Who knows what they told her. Should we turn that person's whole world upside down just for our own curiosity? We talked about it last night for hours. We haven't even told Matthew. We have to now. I just don't know if all this snooping about is worth it. Donna is gone. It won't bring her back. Now, we even have some closure. We know what happened to Donna. We know why she cut us out of her life. We always wondered why she would do that. Now, we understand it was because of the rape and the pregnancy. She was too upset to tell us. At least she had Adam Weaver. I think I will always feel awful she didn't feel she could talk to us, even to her own twin."

"I guess there really is no perfect choice," Mrs. Dindle said.

"Sam and I don't know what will happen when we tell Matthew. How do you tell someone that they are a product of rape? The only father he ever knew was Russ. It's really an awful story," Sarah said.

"Yes, it truly is," Terry said. She wondered if Bruce would want them to tell Matthew. Maybe Matthew would hate Bruce. They were all coming to terms with it. There was no going back now. Three people were now dead because of it.

"I hate to bring this up," Terry said. "I was just thinking that three people are now dead because of that night. At least it seems that way, at the moment. Maybe the best thing to do is to do nothing until we know who the murderer is, or murderers are, whatever the case may be."

"That's probably the smartest suggestion of all," Sarah Wiggins said.

Rose patted Terry's hand and smiled.

The meals were as perfect as Nannie's Place itself. The food made it clear why the diner was so packed. Because they knew Walter wasn't keen on stopping on the way home, the members of the group took turns going to the bathroom. As they waited for the check, it was Dottie's turn to go. Most of the restaurant had cleared out. It was probably the lull before dinner. Terry was amazed at Nannie's energy. Terry thought about the teahouse and imagined she would need a nap before dinner if they kept the same hours as Nannie. Did Nannie have a life? Terry eyed Dottie's empty seat and remembered the Gas-X in her purse. Before they got in the van, she'd quietly offer Dottie a "Listerine" strip. She needed to smuggle them back to Shannon. Maybe not.

After the check was paid, Maude said, "Gosh, I hope Dottie is okay. She's been awhile."

Terry realized that Mrs. Despard was right. "I'll go check," Terry offered. "Unless you think she'll be embarrassed."

"If I were ill, I'd rather be embarrassed than stuck in that bathroom, sick," Rose ventured.

Terry got up and headed to the back. The bathroom was in a small alcove. You couldn't really see it from the restaurant. Besides the two bathrooms, there was a room marked "employees only" and the back door. For a small diner, it was a great set-up. Terry went into the alcove and knocked on the "Ladies" door. It swung open. There was no one there. Terry peeked out the back door, thinking Mrs. Dindle went outside to the car. There was the van, but no Mrs. Dindle. Did they lock the van?

"Is the van locked?" Terry asked, returning to the table.

"Yeah, why?" Walter asked.

"Mrs. Dindle isn't in the bathroom and I didn't see her out back. I was wondering if she could be in the van."

"What do you mean, she isn't in the bathroom?" Rose asked. "Where else could she be?"

"That's my question," Terry said.

"Did you check the other bathroom? Maybe she got confused," Maude suggested.

"While you go check the other bathroom, I'll go check around outside," Walter said. "Maybe she's just standing somewhere we can't see her."

Terry went back and looked around. Both bathroom doors were ajar. Terry was relieved. She didn't like the idea of checking the men's room. It just seemed wrong to her, even though it was a one-seater. Walter came in through the back door. "I just walked around the place. She isn't outside," he said.

They went back to the group. "Dottie would never just leave and wander off," Rose said. "It isn't like her at all. She has to be here."

They all stared at each other. The diner was not that big. They stood at the front door, looking around.

"Is something wrong?" the hostess asked.

"Well, we're not quite sure," Walter said. "Our friend is missing. She just went to the bathroom, but she isn't there now and we're trying to figure out where in blazes she got to."

Before the hostess could answer, a scream ricocheted through the diner. It was coming from the alcove. Terry took off running.

When she got there, the little space was filled with waitresses, waiters, and Nannie herself. Terry couldn't see what everyone was looking at. "Someone better call the police," Nannie barked.

Terry's heart was racing. She could barely stand. She shoved two waitresses out of the way. *Oh, please, dear God, don't let her be dead,* Terry whispered as she pushed a waiter aside so she could see. There, in the closet marked "employees only," was an unconscious Mrs. Dindle, blood trickling down the side of her face. She was sitting propped up against the wall with mops and brooms surrounding her. Her mouth was duct-taped. On her lap, scribbled on a napkin, were the words, "Back Off!" It was too much. Terry turned quickly and vomited onto the waiter's shoes.

***

Karen had a headache the size of Texas. Tea would not shut up. For the last hour, the blasted bird had jumped and flapped around his cage, screeching, "Knock knock. Who's there? Oh, crap." Some of the customers were offended, others couldn't stop laughing. Occasionally, he changed to, "Don't rock the boat. I told you, don't rock the boat! Hellooooo, listen to the birdie, don't rock the boat." At first, it was amusing. It was a nice change from "Crown the kings! Jingle those bells! French hens." But after an hour of listening to him screech, enough was enough. Karen wondered what roasted macaw might taste like.

"What's wrong with Tea?" Shannon asked, grabbing an order from the pass-through "I've never heard him like this."

"Who knows? He might miss Terry. All I know is that he's driving me crazy."

"Normally, he's an attraction, but today, he's a *dis*traction. The customers can hardly hear each other over his noise. Anna said she can hardly hear to take orders."

Shannon's cell phone rang. She set down her tray on the pass-through and looked at the ID. "It's Rose," she told Karen. "That's odd."

Karen watched as Shannon answered her phone. "Rose? What's the—I can't understand you, calm down."

Every muscle in Karen's body tightened.

"Hospital? What? Oh, no! Should I come?"

Karen saw Shannon go pale.

"Okay, okay. Just go with my mother. Don't worry about here. Call me as soon as you—yeah, bye."

"What is it?" Karen said, her body shaking.

"Someone attacked my mother," Shannon said.

"Sit," Karen barked, pointing to the kitchen. She grabbed Shannon's tray and delivered the food.

Anna was just dropping off some dishes. She looked at Shannon and stopped. Karen came up behind her. "Someone attacked Mrs. Dindle, that's all I know." The two women went into the kitchen and sat at the table by Shannon.

"What happened?" Karen asked.

"I don't really know. All I understood, because Rose was crying so hard, was that my mom was attacked somewhere and she's in an ambulance on her way to the hospital."

"Listen to the birdie!" Tea screeched again. "Knock, knock, who's there? Oh, crap. Don't rock the boat, baby!"

CHAPTER 21

It was a little past two in the morning when the minivan pulled into the driveway of the teahouse. Greg and Tom were the first ones out the door, but Shannon pushed them aside and ran to the van. Terry and Walter Nissan helped a frail and shaking Mrs. Dindle out of the front seat.

"Mom," Shannon said, her voice quivering. "I guess this proves I can't let you out of my sight for a moment."

"It's okay, Shannon," Dottie said. "It happens on crime shows all the time. It was my Nancy Drew moment." She patted Shannon's hand.

"Let's get you home," Greg said, beginning to gently assist her.

"Not until I've had my chance to tell everyone my story," Dottie snapped. "I always miss out on the fun. This is my moment of fame."

Terry looked at Shannon who rolled her eyes. They watched Mrs. Dindle walk carefully into the teahouse with Greg and Tom on either side. Henry was holding the door open. "I hope we did the right thing, bringing her home," Terry said. "The hospital really wanted to keep her, but she was adamant she wanted to come home. She was having no part of staying there. I tried to explain that the stitches in her head showed she got a hard conk and we were worried about a concussion," Terry explained.

"It's okay. There's a nurse from Fair Meadows who's coming over between three and three-thirty. Tom made some phone calls and found out about her. She does private duty on the side. She's going to be at the house and keep an eye on my mother so I can sleep. There's another woman coming at eleven tomorrow morning. It'll give me peace of mind."

"Wow, isn't that expensive?" Terry asked.

"Probably, but Tom and Bruce are paying for it. They insisted. Tom says he lives with his mother and has no life." Shannon laughed. "He said he'd be glad to spend the money. Bruce said that he appreciates what they are doing. She got injured looking for his child. Don't say anything to Karen, but I think Bruce has money. I also think he really likes Karen. I admit, he's growing on me. When Mr. Wiggins got here a while ago to pick up Mrs. Wiggins, Bruce tried to lay low, you know, fade in the background, but Mr. Wiggins went and talked to him."

Terry, suddenly aware of how drained she was, said, "I think they're in shock. Both their lives have been turned upside down. It'll take time. Let's go inside and get this over with. I just really want to go to sleep."

"Greg said he talked to you and my mother doesn't know who hit her. Did that change on the ride back?" Shannon asked.

"No, not really. She says she just remembers feeling sad."

"Feeling sad?"

"That's what she says. The bathroom door opened and she thinks she heard another door open and that's all she remembers. She doesn't remember who opened the bathroom door, and she was hit from behind, so she didn't see who hit her."

Shannon was quiet for a moment. "That would make at least two people involved," she said. "That's scary. I can't figure out why she would feel sad. She's probably just confused."

Terry, hand on the doorknob to the teahouse, said, "Yes, I agree, there are at least two people involved. I believe one hundred percent that someone in that diner knows the Frenchions. There's no other explanation."

As they walked in, Terry heard Mr. Wiggins saying, "Sarah, I'll call the attorney in the morning and find a private investigator. You're right, they have to be somewhere."

"Any other news?" Rose asked.

"Unfortunately, no," Greg said. "The gun seems to be a dead end. No pun intended. The Weavers never gave it a second thought after Adam died. Adam's sister, Mandy, swears that Adam told her he gave it to Donna before they graduated. Mandy says that Adam wanted Donna to be able to sleep without worrying someone was going to come at her in the middle of the night. At the time, Mandy had no idea what Adam was talking about. When she tried to ask him about it, he told her to mind her own business. That's all she knows. The Wiggins are adamant that they never saw a gun."

"Donna probably took it with her when she moved," Sarah Wiggins said. "If we had found a gun, we would have confronted Donna. We had no reason to think something was wrong."

"That brings us right back to the Frenchions," Tom added. "Donna probably had the gun when she lived with them. When she died, they probably kept it."

"Three French hens," Mr. Tea squawked.

"Oh my stars," Rose blurted out. "I told you that bird was psychic. He's been trying to tell us about the Frenchions!"

Karen rolled her eyes. "Rose, I'm sure it's a coincidence. Relax. He's a bird. A wonderful bird, but a bird, nonetheless."

"Book 'em, Danno," Tea said.

"It's just random phrases," Karen said.

"Hotel California," Tea squawked, hopping about.

"See," Karen said. "He's just a bird."

"Foolish pride," said Tea.

"Anyway," Karen interjected. "Greg, what else were you going to say?"

"We watched the hotel security tapes over and over. We watched every floor. There's nothing. At least that we can see. Thankfully, Winston has agreed to take a look at them and see if something strikes him. He'll do that tomorrow."

"Winston!" exclaimed Terry. "Why would Winston help out after what he was put through?"

Tom explained. "He says that if he were the police, he would have suspected him, too. After all, he is the security contractor."

Tom's phone vibrated and he looked at it. "Okay, Mrs. Dindle, your nurse has arrived. Home you go. We can have another powwow tomorrow night."

"Henry, did you get us another night at the hotel?" Rose asked.

"Didn't need to. Bruce called a contractor friend of his. He fixed enough of the bedroom so that no cold air is coming in. He's going to be talking to the insurance company. They came out today, too. He was there when they came to inspect the room. The adjuster gave him the okay to start working on it. It seems they've done business before."

Rose turned to Bruce. "Thank you so much." She squeezed his hand.

Bruce looked at her sheepishly. "Let's remember, Mrs. Sanders, the fire bomb was meant for me. I owe you."

Rose, clearly not knowing what to say, just nodded. As Henry was leading Rose to the door, Terry thought she caught him exchanging looks with Mr. Wiggins and

Mr. Nissan. Terry wondered if they were up to something. What could it be? Well, if they were, she would find out about it in the morning. Right now, she was too tired to care.

When the alarm went off at nine o'clock, Terry wanted to smack it across the room. She lay in bed, thinking. This was all getting to be too much. The buried treasure mystery, along with the ghost during the summer had been fun. It was also stressful. Now this. She thought about the teahouse. Karen, Shannon and Anna had made scones and teacakes the day before after the teahouse closed. It had given them something to do while they were waiting on news about Mrs. Dindle. Terry wondered if having some things made ahead would make things easier on a daily basis. She liked getting up early and making things fresh for the day, but perhaps it was wise to be prepared for emergencies. She made a mental note to discuss it with Karen.

Her phone gently vibrated. She had a text. Picking it up, she realized it was from Rose. Wow, Rose didn't text. She was getting bold. Terry looked at the message.

"Cany fund Henrt."

Terry frowned. "Henrt" must mean Henry. What's "cany fund"? Another buzz from the cell phone.

Blasted phone. "I ment Cany find Henrg. Ban gpmg."

Terry giggled. She called Rose.

"I hate that blasted phone," Rose snapped upon answering. "I wanted to say that I can't find Henry. The van is gone."

"Didn't he leave you a note?" Terry asked, getting out of bed.

"He left a note on the counter, saying he was getting together with Walter Nissan and Sam Wiggins for breakfast. Breakfast, my foot! They're up to something. Mark my words."

"Relax, they're probably discussing what to tell the private detective."

"What if something happens and he has another attack?"

"Aunt Rose, he's with two very level-headed men. He'll be fine. Are you dressed?"

"No, I'm way off my game today. I just woke up. Imagine that. Normally, I'm up bright and early. Of course, I don't normally keep such late hours. I must be exhausted not to hear Henry sneak off."

Before she could babble on, Terry interjected. "Just get dressed and come over here." Why did she say that? Why, oh, why? Karen would shoot her.

"Well, hmmm, yes, I suppose I can do that. Perhaps I can help you girls. I need to keep busy. You know what they say about idle hands. You do know—"

"Gotta go, Aunt Rose. I need to get ready myself. Don't rush. I don't want you to upset your delicate constitution." Delicate constitution? *Where in the world did that come from?* Terry asked herself. She hung up the phone and headed for the shower. It was going to be an extremely long day.

By the time Aunt Rose made her appearance, it was ten-thirty. When Rose walked in, Karen gave Terry the death glare.

"Hello, my darlings. I'm sure you must be exhausted, too. What can I do to help?"

"Actually, we're in good shape," Karen said. "Shannon, Anna and I did some baking after the shop closed yesterday. I knew we were going to have a long night."

"Oh, dear me, yes. Have you heard the forecast?"

"No, why?" Karen asked, frowning.

"There's a storm coming. I hope Henry gets back before the snow starts."

"Where did Henry go?" Karen asked.

Rose looked at Terry, a look of shock on her face. "Didn't Terry tell you? He's off with Walter Nissan and Sam Wiggins. I know they're up to something."

"Hmm, they were in the corner, talking quietly last night before Terry and Shannon came in. They looked serious, but I didn't think much about it. I wonder what they're up to."

Rose sat down at the table. She wrung her hands. "I don't like this. He isn't answering his phone. He does that when he wants privacy. He says he forgot it was off. Boloney! Sometimes I could wring that man's neck. Well, I guess I need to go home."

"Go home? You just walked in," Terry said.

"I know, but this could mean another mystery council meeting for tonight. I need to be prepared."

"Sit right back down," Karen said. "You look exhausted. We can meet here. I can order pizza or something."

Rose, who plunked back down on command, said, "Pizza won't be delivered if the weather is bad."

"If the weather is bad, there won't be a meeting," Terry said.

Rose frowned. "I suppose."

"Come help me set some tables," Karen said. "It will take your mind off your troubles."

Terry poured another cup of coffee. She decided she wouldn't mind if there was a storm. Perhaps they would close early. She just wanted sleep.

It was twelve-fifteen when Henry came strolling in. In his wake were Walter Nissan and Sam Wiggins. The teahouse was quiet. It appeared the pending storm had kept people at home. Terry didn't even see cars across the street at the shops.

"Where have you been?" Rose asked, clearly perturbed.

"Walter has a friend who was a principal for the high school where the Frenchion kids went. He moved about two hours from here. We went and picked up some old yearbooks," Henry said, holding up two books. "The Frenchions are in here, but they don't look familiar to us," he said, shaking his head.

"Wait, I have pictures in my purse from yesterday," Terry said. "I forgot all about them." She got her purse and produced the pictures. The women sat down and the men hovered behind them. They looked at each picture.

"Henry, why didn't you just tell me? I worried all day!" Rose snapped.

"I didn't want to say anything until I knew for sure we got the yearbooks," Henry explained.

"Now, that one there, Marion," Mr. Wiggins said, pointing. "I'm pretty sure she's the one who brought us Matthew. She said her name was Denise, but," he flipped back a number of pages, "this is Denise. I don't recognize her."

"Why would she lie about who she was?" Terry asked.

"I don't know. I'm going to show Sarah. Maybe she'll say I'm wrong."

"What about the boy, Arnold?" Terry asked.

They flipped through a few more pictures and found his senior picture. Terry stared at it.

"He looks familiar to me," she said. "It's that smile. It's the chipped tooth in the front. See, the cuspid, that fang-like tooth. He seems to purposely smile so that the tooth is almost hidden."

Karen peered at the picture. "Yeah, maybe. I agree he looks familiar, but I'm not remembering from where."

"Was he at the reunion?" Henry asked.

"I suppose he could have been someone's date," Karen said. "Terry, do you remember him from the registration table?"

Terry thought back. She closed her eyes. She was so tired, she could barely think. "I don't think so. Let's call Greg. He might recognize him." Terry took out her phone and started to text.

"I'm going to get Sarah," Sam said.

Just then, Shannon walked in. "Well, did you forget to invite me to the party?" she asked.

"No, we're looking over some yearbooks Uncle Henry and friends went and picked up this morning. How's your mother?"

"She's in a little pain. The nurse has her resting. She probably should have stayed in the hospital, but she's stubborn. Thankfully, Tom and Bruce got those nurses. Now, what's this about yearbooks?"

"I know a guy who was a principal at the high school out there," Walter explained. "We've stayed in touch. He even does the Santa gig with me this time of year. Like me, he kept a yearbook for every year he was principal. Come take a look."

Shannon sat and looked at the picture of Arnold that Karen pointed to. "Does he look familiar to you, Shannon? Terry and I think we might have seen him, but we can't place him."

Shannon looked at it and shook her head. "No, but do you mind if I look through it?"

"Go right ahead," Henry said.

Mr. Wiggins left, saying he'd be back shortly. Terry was glad they had made some chicken salad and egg salad for sandwiches. At least they could offer people something to eat. She doubted it would get busy now. It was almost one o'clock. The bell above the door jingled and Greg and Tom walked in.

"That was fast," Terry said.

"We were over at the hotel. We wanted to look over Bruce's room, the dumb waiter and the garage. On our way back, I got your message."

"Speaking of the hotel," Karen said. "We need to pick up the decorations. The front desk called yesterday, asking if we still wanted them."

"Oh, rats," Terry said. "I forgot all about those."

"Right there!" Shannon blurted out triumphantly.

Terry looked and saw her pointing to a picture of a group of people on a stage.

"It's the smile," Shannon said, flipping back to the senior photo. "I didn't catch it the first time. I know I've seen that smile. I can't seem to place it, though."

"It's that tooth in the front, isn't it?" Terry said. "The chipped one."

"Yeah," Shannon said, nodding. "I wish I could place where I've seen him."

"Greg, did we see this guy come by the reception table?" Terry asked. "He would have been someone's date."

Greg picked up the yearbook and carefully studied the picture. Tom stood next to him and looked as well. After a minute or so, Greg turned to Tom. "I got nothin'. You?"

"Nope, I don't recognize him."

"Yes," said Shannon. "Yes, yes, yes." She thumped her hand on the table. "I'm sure I've seen him."

"At the reunion?" Tom asked.

Shannon thought for a moment. "Not necessarily. It could have been somewhere else."

"Okay," said Karen. "Where have we been together? If all three of us think we've seen him, where have we been?"

"Oh, no," Rose gasped.

"What?" everyone asked in unison.

"If the three of you recognize him, he must be a customer here."

Everyone was quiet as they let that sink in.

"I don't think so," Terry finally said. "There are a limited number of men who come through here. The ones I don't know are tourists. I don't remember a male tourist coming here a number of times; enough that I would recognize him, anyway. What about you two?" she asked Karen and Shannon.

"Yeah, I agree. I don't think he's a customer," Karen said.

The bell over the door rang again and the Wiggins came in. Sarah ran to the table. Walter showed her the pictures as Sam stood behind her. "That's definitely the woman who came to the house," Sarah said, pointing to the picture of Marion Frenchion. "I'm sure. I don't know why she lied about her name, but she's the one. They're too young in the pictures we got yesterday. They were kids. These high school pictures are much better."

"This is so frustrating," Terry said. "Can I keep these yearbooks? I want to try drawing Arnold and making him older. Maybe it will jog my memory."

"Sure," Walter said. "My friend said he's in no rush to get them back. I see him at the children's hospital at Christmas time. Like I said, he's part of the Santa brigade. Take as long as you need."

"Well, since it's completely quiet today," Terry said. "I want to go to the hotel and pick up the decorations. Shannon, can you help me?"

"I'll help," Greg said. "We can take your car. Tom can take the squad car back to the precinct. Is that okay with you?" Greg asked Tom.

"Yeah, not a problem," Tom said. "I'll give your regards to Thumhart."

***

"It's nice to have a few minutes to ourselves," Greg said, turning to Terry.

"No kidding. Who would think picking up decorations would turn out to be a hot date?" Terry giggled. "Thanks for driving. I hate driving in snow; even if it's just starting."

"Not a problem," Greg said.

"I'm turning my cell phone off for the next hour or so," Terry said, holding it up. "Nothing's going to happen that I need to know about. I'll give you my uninterrupted time."

"That's a good idea. Turn mine off, too. I'm off duty. You know, I hope we can solve these murders by Christmas."

"I never really thought about it," Terry said. "But it would certainly make things quieter."

"I think it would be a nice gift to the Wiggins if they could find out what happened to their granddaughter," Greg added.

"If they find the granddaughter, Bruce will suddenly have two children. Hey, if it hasn't started snowing hard by the time we leave here, let's go look at trees or something. I don't want to rush back," Terry said.

"That sounds great," Greg said, pulling into the semicircle in front of the hotel. "Stay here, I'll run in," he said.

"They should have them ready," Terry explained. "I called and told the girl at the front desk we were coming."

In a few minutes, Greg was back. "The manager said to drive around back to the loading dock. He'll help us put them in the trunk."

As Greg drove into the garage for the hotel, Terry was surprised at how few cars there were. Of course, it was during the week. It would probably be full in another few days. She spotted the manager waving at them from one of the loading docks. Greg backed the car in. They got out and walked up the stairs to the dock where they met the manager.

"Why doesn't Terry stand down by the car and you and I can hand her the boxes?" Greg suggested.

"Yes, sounds like a plan. Let me make sure the door is secure," the manager said, pulling the lever so the door closed. He smiled at them.

That smile. The chipped cuspid. Fear ran through Terry like an electric current. Now, she knew where she'd seen the smile she recognized in the yearbook. The manager was Arnold Frenchion. Terry turned to run, but the door was almost all the way down. Greg look at her, confused, as the manager pulled out a gun.

In a split second, Greg pulled his gun. Frenchion grabbed Terry and pulled her in front of him, the gun to her head. She forced herself not to panic. She kept her eyes on Greg.

"Let me introduce myself, Detective. I am Arnold Frenchion. I understand you've been looking for me."

Terry wanted to distract him. Maybe Greg could get off a shot.

"Why now, Arnold? What's the point? Donna's dead," Terry said.

Frenchion didn't respond. Instead, he simply said, "Detective, throw down your gun. Killing your girlfriend is no problem for me. I have nothing else to lose. "

As Greg complied, Frenchion tightened his hold on Terry.

"I've waited a long time for this," Arnold Frenchion said. "I couldn't believe my luck when the reunion committee booked this hotel. Finally, I could pay back the people who hurt Donna. She could finally be avenged."

"Where's her daughter?" Greg asked.

"Safe. Away from here."

Terry saw Greg suddenly look down. He seemed focused on Arnold's shoes. What was Greg thinking? Then she thought she saw a shadow pass by the door connecting the loading platform to the hotel. It was quick. The door was only open a sliver and the light dulled for only a second. Was someone out there? Should she yell for help?

She looked at Greg. He shook his head and said, "I can't believe you killed three people over this. Do you think that's what Donna wanted? I don't."

Terry realized Greg was shaking his head to tell her not to do anything. He was looking down to make sure he didn't look at the door. He'd seen the shadow, as well. Now, her back was to the door.

"You have no idea what that night did to Donna. My sister met her at the clinic. Donna was a young eighteen-year old girl, alone and frightened. My sister was the receptionist. Over time, she got to know Donna. She brought her home." Arnold looked down, following the line of Greg's vision. He moved forward and kicked the gun away.

Terry felt his balance shift as he kicked the gun. She slammed her heel backward, catching him in the shin. He screamed in pain and shoved her forward toward Greg.

There was a bang as the door crashed open and hit the wall. Tom was in the door with a dive and a roll. He came up, gun pointed at Arnold. "Freeze, police!"

Thumhart was now standing in the doorway, gun pointed at Arnold. Officer Burdick was to Thumhart's right with his gun out.

"Okay, okay," Arnold said. He looked completely shocked. He moved away from Terry and Greg. Slowly he began to turn, his gun pointed slightly up. In a split second, he shot himself in the head.

CHAPTER 22

"How in the world did you know?" Terry said to Tom, as Arnold Frenchion was loaded into an ambulance. It was the first moment she felt strong enough to talk. Greg was with Thumhart, conferencing in the corner.

"I didn't. It was Thumhart. He was talking to Winston Barnstead. Winston said the security tape had been tampered with. Someone had erased a few minutes and then taped over it. When Thumhart asked him who else had access, Winston said, 'Just the manager, Arnie.' Greg told Thumhart this morning what happened yesterday. Thumhart took a guess that Arnie was Arnold Frenchion. When we couldn't reach Greg on his cell, I called Shannon. She said the two of you were at the hotel, getting the decorations. Thumhart grabbed me and Burdick. We headed over here, hoping to intercept you. The receptionist said the manager was at the loading dock. We were only behind you by less than five minutes. You must have gone around to the back just as we pulled up."

"Will he live?" Terry asked, nodding to the ambulance.

"Too soon to tell," Tom said. "If he does, he may be a vegetable."

Greg and Thumhart walked up. "We're sending officers over to his last known address," Greg said. "Maybe they can find something that will tell us who's helping him and where Donna's other child is."

Terry looked up at Greg. "What if we never find her? What if she doesn't know we're looking for her? He was the link."

"We have to take it a step at a time," Thumhart said.

Terry nodded. "It would certainly make the Wiggins happy if we can find her."

"Let's get you home," Greg said.

***

Terry and Greg walked into the teahouse to the sound of laughter. Terry realized that no one there knew what had happened at the hotel. The two looked at each other. Terry wondered why everyone was still here. Why didn't they go home? Weren't they tired?

"Hey," yelled Karen over her shoulder. "It's about time you got home. We decided to have a pre-snowstorm party. It might be a day or two until the roads are good again."

Henry stood up. "Come have a seat. Between the teahouse and our house, we're having a smorgasbord." He walked toward them, but he stopped about halfway. "What's wrong?"

Terry just started to cry. How could she tell the Wiggins?

After Greg told the story, everyone was silent for a bit. Terry didn't know what to say. It was Rose who spoke first. "Well, thank God they got to you in time. Although, I'm confused about all of this. It leaves more questions than answers."

"I need to call Bruce," Greg said. "I don't want him to see it on the news first." He looked at his cell and frowned. "Oh, yeah, it's off," he said, pushing a button on the side. A moment later, the phone rang in his hand. He answered it. "Hey, Tom." No one spoke as Greg listened. "Okay. Keep me posted." He shut his phone. "When they got to the address they had for Arnold, no one was there. A neighbor said Arnold lived there with three women: his sister, his wife, and their daughter. The neighbor believed they all worked at the hotel. Now, if you'll excuse me," he said, heading toward the kitchen. "I really gotta call Bruce."

There was another brief silence as everyone contemplated the swift turn of events. It was Sarah Wiggins who spoke first. "I'll bet his daughter is really my granddaughter."

"Let's not rush ahead of ourselves, Sarah," Sam Wiggins admonished. "Greg just said there's mention of only one sister. The other sister could have the child, or they could have let the child be adopted. We better pray Arnold Frenchion doesn't die. He's the man with the answers."

Terry felt a lump in her stomach as she remembered the last time she saw Arnold Frenchion.

***

"Wow, that was quite the storm," Terry said to Karen. "Can you believe it's been two days of quiet?"

"It hasn't been quiet," Karen said. "We've spent two days with Uncle Henry and Aunt Rose, playing board games and Uno."

"You shouldn't be complaining," Terry said. "You downed quite a bit of Henry's spiked eggnog."

"True, but eggnog or no, I can't sleep. I'm still in shock over this whole thing," Karen said, sipping her coffee.

"Everyone is. Greg called me last night and told me that the last number Arnold called belonged to a cell phone found in the apartment Frenchion lived in. That cell phone was also the number that texted Bobby. Everything in the apartment was wiped clean. Greg also told me that, according to the hotel, a bartender and two housekeepers didn't show up for work the last few days. Everyone else is accounted for. The employment forms showed them as Marion French, Barbara Fields, and Sarah Potter. The police think they have fake IDs. Arnold was able to hire those three without anyone suspecting. They worked at the hotel four months. They had plenty of time to plan."

"It makes sense that one of them was the bartender. It would be easy for her to slip something into Chris's drink," Karen suggested. "It could also explain why Bruce was so woozy that first night. His drink might have been drugged as well."

"Quite true," Terry agreed. "I keep wondering if the young girl Arnold lived with was Donna's daughter. It would make sense that he kept her."

"It might, but then it makes me wonder if the woman he said was his wife really was. If he married, why would he drag her and his daughter into this? I can see one of the sisters wanting to avenge Donna, but an unconnected wife and child?"

"Maybe it was really the two sisters and not a sister and a wife," Terry ventured.

"I hope that young girl isn't Donna's daughter. If she is, she's involved in these murders."

"Then we're right back to wondering who she is," Terry said. "We might never know. Arnold is still in a coma."

"Maybe the Wiggins's private detective can figure it all out. My mind is too boggled," Karen said.

"Don't forget the police are hoping they can find pictures of those women on security tapes from the hotel. Karen, why do you think they wanted to avenge Donna's rape? What difference would it make after all these years?"

"No clue. Maybe Arnold had some bizarre hold over the women."

"I suppose. I keep trying to remember everything Arnold said to us, but I wasn't really concentrating on what he was saying at the time," Terry said.

"How's Greg? The two of you must have been scared to death," Karen said.

"Initially, I was," Terry explained. "But Greg and I realized pretty quickly that someone was on the other side of the door. Neither one of us thought it was the police, though. We were hoping whoever it was knew enough to stay out and just call the police."

"Yeah, the two of you are pretty dang lucky. After this summer, you might want to lay low, little sister. Your luck has got to be running out."

Terry considered this for a moment. Karen had an extremely valid point.

***

It was quite cold and windy the day of Bobby's memorial service. Shantel decided she didn't want a graveside service after the memorial. Maybe something in the spring. Shantel's song for Bobby caused the majority of people to pull out their packet of tissues. Terry and Karen volunteered to cater the luncheon in the church hall. The teahouse being closed due to the weather made that feat easier for them. Almost three feet of snow wasn't a record breaker, but it sure slowed things down. As Terry was setting out another tray of salmon salad sandwiches, she saw Rachelle walk up to Bruce. In her wake was a much younger carbon copy of Bruce. He had the same oval face, nose, build and curly hair. Terry did the math in her head and realized Matthew was almost 20. Terry never realized she was holding her breath until she breathed a sigh of relief as the two men shook hands. Bruce looked scared to death. Terry couldn't make out what Bruce was saying. She was about to turn away when she saw Matthew nod and Bruce hugged him. *Perhaps something good really can come out of this*, she thought.

Chapter 23

Greg's back ached. His muscles were screaming at him. The storm had lived up to its hype. Most of the police force had spent the last twenty-four hours helping those stranded by the snow. He answered his cell. "Mullins."

"Hey," Tom said. "Where are you?"

"Over by Seawater and Sandscrescent; why?"

"The motel, Bays End, is having problems. I called over there 'cause a number of people called, saying they can't get their cars out. The owner is elderly and said his staff hasn't shown up to help shovel. I'm sending some guys out there when they call in. Can you get over there and knock on some doors and let them know we're working on it?"

"Yeah, okay, I guess we're shovel patrol, now. Why call me on my cell? Why not use the radio?"

"If I had Marge use the radio for this, everyone who needs help shoveling would be calling in. People have nothing better to do than listen to their scanners. The bright side is that no one can get out to rob anyone, or go to a bar and slug anyone."

"Good point," Greg said, chuckling. "I should count my blessings. It's better than having a gun pointed at me."

"Oh, yeah, I forgot to tell you, Thumhart says there's no change in Frenchion's condition."

"Wow, I'm surprised he's still hanging in. Although, we have an awful lot of questions to ask him. I'll call you if I run into any problems at the motel. If not, I'll start shoveling and wait for help."

Greg headed over to Bay's End. The roads were extremely narrow. He doubted the town plows had plowed this road within the last twelve hours or so. People were shoveling and snow blowing. With no place to put it, most of the snow wound up back in the street. Greg could see a few brave souls walking toward the small market at the end of the street. They looked like pencil dots on a white sheet of paper. He imagined some of them might even be guests from the motel who were going crazy being cooped up. He saw cars with ski racks filled with skis, but they couldn't even get on the roads to get to the slopes.

He climbed out and stretched. After going to the front desk to let them know help was coming, Greg went out to start knocking. The rooms made a U shape with their blue doors facing the parking lot. The owner had managed to dig out in front of most of the doors. Greg assumed the ones not dug out were unoccupied. The white snow and the white wooden building were almost blinding together. The first two rooms were occupied by couples in their twenties. They were rude and arrogant, just wanting to get out and to the slopes. The third room held a mother with two small children. When Greg told her help was on the way, he thought for a second she might kiss him.

"Oh, thank you so much," she said, tears springing to her eyes." I just don't know how many more episodes of these cartoons I can take!"

He knocked on the fourth door. He could hear someone in there. The curtain parted a bit. He knocked again. "Hello, police," he said forcefully. He wished they'd answer the door. He didn't want to be at this all day. It was still quiet. A flip in his gut told him something might be wrong. He was about ready to go for a key when he heard the lock turn. He stepped to the side and put his hand on his gun. He was steeled for whatever happened. At least he thought he was.

The door opened and she smiled at him. It was actually a smirk, like she was wondering when he'd show up.

"Greg Mullins. Long time no see. Actually, I've seen you, you just didn't see me. Being skilled at stage make-up has its advantages."

It took every bit of training he had to not react. He was staring at a woman who, except for her hair style, was a replica of Rachelle Wiggins. "Donna," he said as casually as he could manage. *Where the heck is that back-up?* he thought.

"If it wasn't for this stupid storm, we'd be long gone."

We'd be long gone. He scanned the room. Both beds were made. He didn't see any luggage.

"Arnold's dead, isn't he?"

Okay, she doesn't know. Use this to your advantage. "No, he's in custody. I thought you knew that. We found you because there's an A.P.B. out for you." He hoped his voice did not betray the lie. His head was abuzz with *Holy cow chips, Donna's alive!*

She studied him. "No. He called and said that if he didn't call back in twenty minutes, we should leave. He said he'd die before he'd let you take him into custody."

"Well, I'm a better shot," Greg said casually. "How could you do that to your parents? They thought you were dead. Didn't you care what you did to your mother?"

"Of course I cared; don't be absurd," she said with a flip of her hand. "How much did Arnold tell you?"

"What Arnold says doesn't matter. Your version may not agree with his." His ears strained for the sound of cars pulling into the motel parking lot.

"Oh, you might as well come in. I'm getting cold, standing here." She sounded like she had just invited him in for tea.

"No, I think perhaps you'd best come with me."

She rolled her eyes. He was shocked. *Really? Three people are dead and I'm inconveniencing her!*

"I have to at least get my purse. I also need to go to the bathroom. You're welcome to check it for windows, detective."

He stepped in, but didn't shut the door. She continued talking.

"Denise took my purse the night of the accident. It not only had the keys, but my wallet. My driver's license still had my parents' address. She was probably high on something. When we saw on the news that the police thought I was dead, Arnold and Marion thought I should just stay dead."

"Why give your parents Matthew?"

"Because he was a boy. He was conceived during that rape. I didn't want to raise a rapist. Sarah stood a chance. She has my aptitude for make-up and disguise. She's really quite talented."

"You didn't want to raise a rapist, but you involved your daughter, whom I'm assuming you named after your mother, in three murders? That sounds a bit convoluted to me, Donna."

Donna smiled. "She has Arnold's sense of justice, I'm afraid. She's come in quite handy. The black angel of death wings and feathers were her idea. Quite imaginative, I think." Donna folded her arms across her chest. "She's an excellent bartender. She was able to drug Bruce's drink and Chris's drink without anyone knowing. Of course, the timing of hitting the lights was tricky. Arnold had a walkie-talkie set up. When she used a certain phrase, he short-circuited the lights in the hotel. He used to be an electrician, you know. Did he tell you that?"

"No, he left that part out, although it does make sense. Where are Marion and Sarah now?" He was stalling for time. He wondered why she was telling him all this. Could someone be in the bathroom? He kept his hand on his gun.

"They made it out ahead of me. They took the other car. I stayed behind to wipe things down. I waited a bit too long, apparently."

"Who was it that attacked Mrs. Dindle in the diner?" Greg asked, wanting to get as much out of her as he could.

"I felt so bad about that. Our costumes that day were amazing. Arnold and Sarah heard you all talking at the bar that night. It was Sarah who introduced the women to caramel apple shots. Mr. Nissan even asked Arnold to have the car delivered to the hotel. Marion and I got a head start on the little group. We looked so much like overweight, middle-aged women that no one recognized us in the diner. We sat only a few tables away from them. It was quite exciting, really. Marion went out the front and I scooted into the bathroom when we saw her getting up to make her little visit. When she knocked on the door, I opened it. I did tell her I was so sorry. I really was. She was startled when I called her Mrs. Dindle. Marion came in the back way, and thonk, night, night, Mrs. Dindle. I hope the poor dear is okay. Is she?"

"You killed three people, one of whom sent money every year to a memorial named after you and set up by your parents, and you feel bad Mrs. Dindle got hurt. Hmmmm, that's interesting."

"Oh, please. Spare me the heartbreaking tales of heroism. They raped me. That big fat oaf of a coach egged them on. When I went to him for help, he laughed at me. Laughed right in my face and said he wanted a paternity test. I was a virgin and he made me out to be a common whore. Well, I got the last laugh, thanks to Arnold." She sat down on the bed.

"You said you needed to go to the bathroom," Greg said, nodding toward the bathroom door.

"Ahh, and so I did," said Donna.

Greg heard a small noise at the door. He turned slightly and saw a woman he did not recognize and a girl who was the spitting image of a younger Mrs. Wiggins. A quick movement caught his eye. He turned and felt his body stiffen completely, and then he felt himself falling. He realized too late that Donna had a Taser gun.

***

"Detective Mullins? Detective?"

He felt nauseated and the room was spinning. Officer Burdick came slowly into focus. He was kneeling over him.

"Did you get them?" Greg asked.

"Get who? There was no one here but you when we got here."

"My radio! Hand me a radio, quickly."

***

"Here we go," said Rose, swishing into the room. "Henry's eggnog for all." She grinned at Greg who was sitting curled up on the couch in front of the fireplace with Terry tucked up under his arm. Terry just wanted to stay there for a few days. Donna could have killed him. First Arnold and now Donna. She thought back to what Karen had said about her luck running out. Maybe she and Greg needed to be more careful. Rose, naturally, invited the Dindles and Tom over. Another crisis, another powwow. Rose was so excited, she even told Terry to bring Tea. "Greg, can I get you anything else?" Rose asked.

"No, no thank you, Mrs. Sanders."

Henry shook his head. "How are the Wiggins taking it?"

"Not very well, I'm afraid. Mr. Wiggins called the private investigator and ended the search. It was the first thing he did. I think he was angry, feeling betrayed. Mrs. Wiggins just cried and stared out the window."

"Do you think they'll be found?" Karen asked.

"Probably. A man in a nearby room in the motel had just finished shoveling out his car. He started it up and they opened the door and threw him out. The car was found a few hours later. Where they went from there, we have no idea. Their pictures are all over the news. However, I do have to say, they must be quite good with disguises. No one recognized Donna at the reunion where she was working as a housekeeper. None of you recognized her and Marion at the diner. Who knows? If Arnold wakes up, he might be able to fill in a few of the blanks," Bruce said. "The thing with the black feathers really did freak me out. I'm a little embarrassed that I fell for it."

"Well, they drugged your drink so you'd be groggy," Greg said. "No one stopped to think that your drink was drugged before you went to bed. Whatever the drug, it made you believe you were really seeing the angel of death."

"I can't believe Donna's still alive," Bruce said, shaking her head. "Of all the scenarios I imagined, that was definitely not one of them. I'm stunned she didn't care if her family thought she was dead. Even worse, she was willing to give away Matthew and turn Sarah into a killer!"

"I think she was dead long before that," Terry surmised. "I think she died the night of the rape. At least the Donna we knew did. She never got help. She shut out her family. Her emotional wound just festered. The sweet and funny person we knew ceased to exist. I suppose I should feel sad for her, but I can't."

"Well," Henry said, "we don't know what role the Frenchions played. They found an emotionally damaged young girl and nursed her anger and hatred. It was a bad situation made worse. We may never really know."

"Yeah," said Tom, "but I sure would like to ask Frenchion a bunch of questions."

"You know, I wish I had recognized her at the diner," Mrs. Dindle said. "I didn't really have much time to think. Although, maybe I did, a little. I remember feeling sad. Maybe that's why." She shrugged. "It's too late now, I suppose."

"Thank God they didn't kill you," Shannon said, shuddering.

"Dottie, we all sat at that table and not one of us suspected a thing. I have wracked my brain, trying to picture which table they sat at," Rose said. "I suppose, for now, we can just concentrate on Christmas."

"Santa's coming to town," Tea added. "Tea and crumpets for Christmas!" Tea rang his bell as everyone laughed.

Terry looked at Rose and guessed she was feeling a bit of a letdown. The woman loved playing sleuth. Nothing like a crisis to perk up Aunt Rose.

"Rosey, I think our detecting days are done," Henry said, winking at Rose.

"Wrong-o, buddy boy," squawked Mr. Tea. "Tea and crumpets for Christmas."

Terry sat up and turned to Karen. "You know, maybe we should learn to make crumpets. Tea and crumpets for Christmas sounds lovely."

THE END

ABOUT THE AUTHOR

 Leslie Matthews Stansfield is the author of MR. TEA AND THE TRAVELING TEACUP, the first book in the Madeline's Teahouse series. She is also the author of a book about the town she lives in. She grew up in Delmar, New York, and credits her friends with developing her imagination. She is a graduate of the University of Hartford and recently received her Masters' Degree from the University of Phoenix in Educational Leadership. She is a math tutor in a public school as well as the Christian Education Director of her church. MR. TEA AND THE BOBBIN' BODY is the second book in the Madeline's Teahouse series. Leslie has four children and eight grandchildren and lives in Windsor Locks, Connecticut.